LIFE
CLOSE
TO THE
BONE

erations if they are allowed to stay buried. For most of his life and through all of his accomplishments John has never been able to dig himself out from under the pressure his mother, Francis, has put on him to prove that she belongs. What will it take, how much can one man take, before it all comes crashing down? Michael Spake writes with an honest voice that instantly draws you in and breathes life to his characters."

-MANDY HAYNES, Editor-in-Chief of *WELL READ Magazine*, author of *Walking the Wrong Way Home, Sharp as a Serpent's Tooth: Eva and Other Stories*, and *Oliver*

"Michael Spake clearly has a story to tell that haunts him. Corporate ethics lawyer John Greenburn's work life unravels and thrusts him into dealing with a troubling relationship, the one he has with his mother."

-BREN MCCLAIN, Author of *One Good Mama Bone*, winner of the French Prix Maya for Best Animal Novel, the Willie Morris Award for Southern Fiction, and the Patricia Winn Award for Southern Literature, published as *Mama Red* in France

"In this thoughtful coming-of-age debut novel, Michael Spake explores the past, reminding us that 'It is forever a part of our experience, and we cannot disown it.' An attorney himself, the author pulls back the curtain on the extraordinary ethical demands and challenges of the vocation in a culture of corporate greed while exploring the complicated and formative dynamics of family and expectations in the American South. Ultimately, this is a powerful story of self-discovery and transformation."

-REBECCA DWIGHT BRUFF, author of *Trouble the Water*

LIFE CLOSE TO THE BONE

A NOVEL

MICHAEL SPAKE

This book is dedicated to the Spake family and especially my wife, Mary Lucia, who has forever told me, "You have a story to share."

Thank you to Cassandra King, Jonathan Haupt, Tim Conroy, and my friends at the Pat Conroy Literary Center for pushing me to find my Great Yes.

Finally, thank you to all the members of the Cardinal Raquet Club in Anderson, South Carolina, all my high school coaches and teammates, and all my college coaches and teammates.

The owl of Minerva takes flight only at dusk.

G. W. F. HEGEL

CHAPTER ONE

On the worn surface of my desk, my iPhone dances with a buzzing noise. Its siren call of my father pierces the veil of my mundane world. He calls now instead of my mother. I decline to answer.

Still, the buzzing makes me fidget with silent restlessness. I squeeze my fists. Unclench. Or try to, anyway. The suffocating weight is too much. Drip by drip, the slow venom from the past seeps into my veins down to the core of my being. Once more, the sharp throbbing pain of memory returns echoing cadences of regret and wounds which have never healed.

Although my tense fingers are stiff, I send a text message to my wife, Clare, a plea meant to rescue me. "Is there a *reason* Dad is calling me? He knows I am at work."

Clare and I did not meet until after college, but twenty-five years of marriage have provided her with plenty of time to witness the relationship I have with my parents, especially my mother—a tempest of passion unleashed upon the world, a force to reckon with. I have never understood my mother's displaced passion, and she has never understood my quiet sensitivity. Worse, no one was more masterful at exercising the power of guilt than my mother, and I, a Southern son, was always unable to resist needing her acceptance and love, at times never refusing a second helping and always ending up ensnared by the thorny embrace of obligation.

My father does not often call me while I am at work. However, each time he does, it signals a storm brewing on the horizon. I dip into my shallow reservoir of coping skills and answer, only to hear, "John, what are you doing?" or he asks me to deal with a minuscule issue my mother is obsessing about and at the point of flying off the handle over. Each call serves as a grim reminder of my mother's constant need to control, like the time I was twenty-two and she confronted me at work because our neighbor saw me buying a case of beer at the local grocery. "Mom, I am an adult. I am getting married next year." She does not care about the alcohol. Her only worry, did somebody she know see me?

Her scripted reply, "I am just so disappointed in you and your poor choices." She knows her words make my heart sink. My father never intervened in our conflicts. He smartly picked his battles, and it was not until I was an adult that I understood why.

I draw a deep breath and return to my office computer, where mindless memos, letters, and emails await. Each does nothing more than justify the existence of others and the soul-sucking corporate world of politics and other man-made intuitions. In this world, smoke and mirrors reign supreme. Solace is only found in small victories, which randomly appear as fleeting moments of hope amid the chaos of reality.

As the chief ethics officer at Cogniv-Pharma, a worldwide pharmaceutical company specializing in memory-loss prevention medicines, I am an attorney with specialized training in regulatory law. My purpose is to serve as the organization's moral compass in a world filled with moral ambiguity. I stand with unwavering resolve as a bulwark against noncompliance, improprieties, and conflicts of interest. I see my role as a noble pursuit as I endeavor to protect the reputation of the organization by instilling a culture of integrity.

The last several years the laudable purpose of my role has been eroded by men of greed who demand I justify their questionable actions to grow profits, all done by exploiting a population more vulnerable than ever. I struggle to survive the cutthroat competition and laissez-faire attitudes of corporate behavior. I no longer grapple with questions of profound morality, those deep cerebral pursuits that once filled my intellect with the greatness of humanity. Instead, I am now a mere solitary voice in the wilderness of profit-making and others see me merely as a pawn in a game devoid of conscience.

Like my mother, I'm a workaholic, a relentless pursuer of perfection, and adept at chameleon-type behavior. In the quiet recesses of my soul, I have always had to be with my mother and her expectations. I've known for a long time what it means to turn from my authentic self. Yet, I have continued to press on and now, I get paid to do it.

I have longed many years to change out of this charade, but I, like most men of a certain age, am weary and lie in defeat to conformity. I remember the time I stood at an intersection of understanding who I am. As a Pisces I felt the pull between two distinct paths. One path, its allure inviting, pulled me in the direction of my creative passions. The other, the well-trodden pragmatic path, pulled toward the material world. Always taught by my mother *what* "to do," I never learned *how* "to do" or *why*. As a result, I blindly stumbled along the pragmatic path, which has led me to a secular reality stripped of authenticity and truth.

That was my fault and today I still blame myself—every day.

Looking into the past, I see how over time the pragmatic path, with its luring goals of money and social standing, has guided me into a dark crater of shadows, much like the dark crater of memories my mother has struggled with since living in the Shoals Mill village as a "linthead" or "white trash," disparaged as a low-paid minimally skilled operative and struggling to survive. These memories entwined with the sudden death of her father all fill a spiritual cemetery of remembrances within my mother that she never speaks about other than when she reminds me, "I was teaching when I heard the ambulance race by the school. I knew it was Daddy, and I knew he was already dead."

These graves, too deep to rise out of, churn undercurrents of sorrowful memories, unleashing relentless and unyielding waves of grief that crash down on all of us.

My parents are offspring of lintheads, a curse that clings to the marrow of each generation from the mill village. It is how they inherited their ancestral conviction and pride. My grandparents and their parents began and ended their lives in the Shoals Mill village, one of many textile mills in upstate South Carolina, where red hills of clay greet the majestic Appalachian Mountains, the clear mountain-fed streams of the French Broad River feed tales of moonshine, and skylines of smoky blue haze and tenuous mist inspire tales of ghosts.

My mother's family never let go of the heartache experience in Shoals Mill. They were determined to survive, even if it meant swallowing a lot of bile. With no outlet, they lived the "rough life." They drank to escape their disappointments and the burdens of mill life. At family gatherings women talked over coffee in the family room and men drank moonshine in the kitchen. Each gathering broke out in a fistfight between the drunken men. Once, a drunk cousin broke a chair over his father's head and killed him. Later, the family bailed the cousin from jail so he could join the family in mourning at the graveside. The next day he was shot by his mother, who mistook him in the middle of the night for a chicken thief.

On other days, wives threatened husbands with the cold steel of a butcher knife and screamed threats of reparations, which echoed throughout the mill village. When neighbors got weary of their relentless tirades, they called the police, who arrived with a patience born of routine and listened to the women's plaintive cries for a better life beyond the grinding of mill life. Yet, long before the distant wail of the policeman's siren faded into the darkness, these same fighting couples found solace in the tangle of lovemaking, a desperate balm of healing. Their lives were a contradictory cycle of passion and bitter hate. The calculus of their life was always fragile, perpetually flirting with the brink of destruction.

Like many mill workers, my parents left to improve the lot of their children, my brother, Will, and me. They remained in town but moved to the better side of the tracks. They turned to a new corporate America for hope. My father drove fifty miles to work at a European tire manufacturer opening operations in North America. Like the earlier mill bosses who found cheap labor from failed farmers, the tire industry found cheap labor from out of work mill hands or those, like my parents, who were seeking to escape the tarnish of their mill heritage. The tire manufacturer claimed it would train my father and take care of his family, just like the mill told generations before him and just like with the mill, time would reveal their "true colors" of deceit.

My mother's parents left the mill before it closed. Leaving the mill somehow makes my mother feel superior to my father, who worked hard and provided much. I remember during arguments my mother always shouting at my father, "You can take the boy out of the mill hill, but you can't take the mill hill out of the boy."

I see my mother's fastidious nature in myself.

Each month, my mother balanced the checking account down to the penny. She sat at the oak roll-top desk, my grandfather's desk from his house on the mill, with her ledger, a calculator, and a box with a copy of each check written during the month. Each month my brother and I listened as my mother telephoned my dad at work. "How the hell did you forget to record the check you wrote at the grocery store? How did you record the incorrect amount?" Each call ended with her saying, "If you cannot get things right you might as well move back to the mill hill." This, her intentional insult aimed at my father like twisting a dull knife into his back. White trash, failure, and uneducated are never terms of endearment.

As a child listening, I reminded myself, *I do not want that to ever be me.*

Every day my mother would say to me, "Do you not see the sacrifices we are making for you?" She would sew her own clothes and patch holes in our sneaker soles with "Shoe Goo." She'd travel to outlets, never paying full price for a name brand item of clothing. Unable to afford antiques, my mother would refinish old furniture and make curtains to inspire a feel of European elegance in our house. Every day my mother would remind me, in her ways, where we come from.

My mother's memory of her mill village heritage, full of pain and sadness. It is a blight upon her being. Rather than reconcile and heal, she, like members of other mill families, became a master at forgetting. I always felt this type of intentional forgetting had to be one of the most pitiful of human abilities. Shame and misinformation fuel her fire of forgetting and constant quest to leave the past and the mill heritage that constantly whispers reminders of her inadequacies.

Hiding her mill heritage means living a guarded life walled off from everyone and everything that may pierce her fragile veil of secrecy. My mother has, my whole life, kept everyone from her interior, especially the deep pain that wrapped her heart. Her inescapable past eats at her. She swallows her feelings, bitter pills of sorrow and regret, and searches for ways to rise above the crushing weight of the past. No matter, it stays with her.

The past is never really forgotten. It is always alive, and it stays with my mother and chafes her wounds. This leaves her in a perpetual state of distress, living until the sagging undercurrents of her grief fester and explode.

My mother's naked despair of the mill shaped my brother, Will, into a warrior with a stout heart, who was always ready for battle. I never understood his ravenous appetite for independence. Unlike me, conflict did not bother him. Will thrived on confrontation with my mother. He was bold, never longing for her approval, even her opinion. Her violent reactions never pierced his armor of thick skin. Unlike me, he did not need a shield for protection. Each battle with her was a victory for his independence. Worse, each battle left my mother feeling unloved and unappreciated, so I was always there to defend her at all costs. I was her co-conspirator, shedding tears my brother, too stoic, would never allow.

As a child, then a teenager, then a young man, I always thought it would get easier, but it doesn't, and nothing demonstrates this to me more than these midday calls from my father.

My purpose in life was change, the heavy burden of helping my mother forget the past. This is why she called me "her serendipity." I was meant to help her sever the past forever, and my power to do this was an ability, beyond others', to play tennis. This idea that I was gifted and therefore would be blessed was an unconscious and unchosen decree, not a gift.

Of course, I am not a professional tennis player. I am a lawyer. I failed her in this, too, never practicing law at a large corporate downtown firm, but instead embracing the ethics of organizational values and integrity.

My mother embraced me playing tennis and thrust it upon me in such a passionate manner it became an unchosen purpose for me, a beacon to lift me out of the mire of other own past. She considered tennis a passageway, a conduit to also elevate her above the drudgery of her current reality. She viewed it as a gift God gave especially to me. This is how I became ensnared in her web of obligation. Every forehand, every volley, and, especially, every win served as a testament to unyielding purpose.

For me, tennis was not a sport, but a mandate in life diverting me from the creative passions that stirred my soul. It was a storm of confusion and self-doubt, fueled by my mother's punctuated disappointment and compelled by her discontentment as the racket in my hand became a shackle tethering us together.

Later, I realized tennis offered my mother a reflecting pool. Winning reflected her rise from the mill and losing served as a reminder of her bitter failures from the past. This meant there could be no escape as my own feelings festered beneath, raw and unhealed.

I carried this heavy burden as best as I could, but it was too great. I never learned to manage my own feelings, which always fester and ooze like a scratched pimple. This turned me into a powder keg, and I exploded on the tennis court with raw emotional outbursts, leaving behind only broken rackets to match my broken spirit.

Before tennis, I was a six-year-old naturalist, an explorer of earthly things, digging for rocks, finding salamanders by creeks, and following box turtles in the grassy backyard. I belonged outside, in the woods, or by a lake. Unaware of the true world surrounding me, my soul lived in a world of unspoiled virtue and my innocence was as simple and pure a packet of Dixie Crystals sugar.

This was a time when there was no competition. Sure, when we played, Will, because he was the older brother, was always the major character. For example, I never got to be the Lone Ranger, and I was always Robin and Will was Batman, but I did not care. We were always partners in our adventures, which meant I was always loyal and by his side and he always protected me.

In the middle of our neighborhood was a large, wooded lot full of intrigue. Once, when the city trimmed the pine trees around the power lines, Will and I used the large green branches to make a lean-to. There we had a fort to store the treasures we found.

We collected pieces of mica dug from the banks of red clay near the street and carried plastic bags to fill with bird feathers, dried bugs, and the occasional snakeskin. When we were not scavenging for treasures left behind by animals, we lay in the backyard and looked for four-leaf clovers, then made necklaces from the clovers' white flower heads. When there was nothing to find, we took our matchbox cars to the fort and created small towns, using sticks and small pieces of glass Coca-Cola bottles to make houses.

We also dedicated nights to the fort. Each night in our backyard grove of pine trees, we filled mason jars with lightening bugs. We took them to the fort as lanterns in hopes of lighting our small habitat. Little did we know how these self-illuminating beetles projected their healing energy onto us, helping us light our own souls.

Some of my other first memories of this time include our neighbor, Mr. Shook. He was a gentleman, about ten years older than both my parents, and the type of neighbor every young child needs. He was a kind person. Each time he saw me, he invited me over to his backyard, where he had a magical vegetable garden with an assortment of fruits and vegetables. I watched Mr. Shook cradle everything he planted and tame the wild weeds attempting to invade his sanctuary. His garden attached him to the earth and comforted him when he was sad, always slowing down life and putting it into proportion. It was his own world and he openly shared it with me by teaching me how to identify each vegetable. On special days, he allowed me to pick strawberries or pull carrots.

For me, the garden inspired my imagination to roam free. I pretended to be Beatrix Potter's Peter Cottontail each time Mr. Shook let me pull a carrot or radish. I was Tom Thumb when I first tasted a plum from his tree, and I was Farmer Green Jeans when we sat on his back porch and shelled butter beans. Each trip Mr. Shook thanked me by giving me something from the garden and, like everything I garnered from the neighborhood, I enjoyed it in the lean-to fort.

Before I started the second grade my parents moved out of the house my grandfather built before his fatal heart attack. My interest as a young naturalist grew when I discovered how our new neighborhood had two ponds full of fish, families of mallards, and an assortment of snakes, frogs, and turtles. In addition, two small, spring-fed creeks leading into one of the ponds served as boundaries for our yard. In the creeks, I found salamanders, and I watched the life cycle of tadpoles. At the pond, I fished and fed bread to the ducks.

During this time in my life, there was no tennis, so every day I grabbed my simple Zebco 33 rod and reel, my small tackle box filled with plastic worms, and a bucket and headed to the pond. On Saturdays, I packed a peanut butter sandwich and fished until late afternoon. At the end of the day, after fishing for hours, my mother drove me to her mother's house. There, my grandmother, my mother's mother, Hazel, gave me twenty-five cents for every bream, fifty cents for every catfish, and one dollar for every largemouth bass. Usually, this provided enough income to restock my tackle box with new worms and lures for the following Saturday.

Many days, I long to be that young boy innocently exploring the pond, unencumbered by expectations and finding the genuine of life.

I began to feel this way long before true adulthood. But, even then, the obstacles blocking my desire to honor those truest parts of myself were insurmountable. I must now accept those days are forever lost.

From a young age, even people beyond the confines of my family identified me with tennis and, like my family, they saw my ability as a tennis player as a divine gift. There was no room for my own desires or the things that truly interested me. It was more than people misunderstanding me. Eventually, tennis became a lonely endeavor. I felt its solitary pursuit disconnect me from everything meaningful.

Even today family members lament, "John never played up to his talent and always took his gift for granted." They never saw my inner turmoil or understood how nature, music, and books fulfilled something profound inside me, far more than tennis ever could.

Tennis also meant having very few friends. I was always expected to despise and even taunt every opponent. I detested this because it made me feel like a jerk. When I protested, my mother always dismissed me, "You are too sensitive. You need to get tougher like your brother."

I did not attend parties with school friends; music, reading, and writing were my only oasis, a refuge from the relentless demands of tennis. However, this oasis vanished each time my mother deemed music and reading distractions from my true purpose, tennis.

As time passed, I grew to resent tennis, realizing my talent was built on hate and not the beauty of the game or the love for it. Tennis became a source of shame and unworthiness, and today I am plagued by the constant need to apologize and seek forgiveness, another trait of the compliant Southern son feeling forever trapped in an endless cycle of shame and self-doubt.

During my years playing tennis, I needed help, more than a Band-Aid or pat on the back. I needed true support; the kind you may receive from a professional counselor. But not in family. My family believed seeking help from others was a sign of weakness. They believed all feebleness must be overcome by self-discipline; otherwise, you asked Jesus.

As a result, I heard daily admonitions: "Work harder, practice more, concentrate more; you have so much talent but no idea how to use it. It's a sin." As a result, like my mother, I learned to embrace my reality by burying everything deep within myself.

Today, I reflect on how my mother, and I live close to the bone—everything untold, everything meant to be forgotten, especially her past, about which I know hardly anything at all

The iPhone continues to buzz. My father is my mother's voice now.

Years of guilt pull at me to answer it. At the same time, my mind begs me to let it go as I sit at the desk of a job I hate, and in an industry which is consuming me, just like tennis.

CHAPTER TWO

Beside my dancing iPhone sits a federal subpoena addressed to me, John Greenburn, Cogniv-Pharma Chief Ethics Officer. It glares at me. I squint my eyes and, in my blur, I see the fury of my mother's eyes when I was losing on the tennis court, her unspoken rage seethes through the lines on the page. Without opening it, I also know it pulses the same anger, her anger.

"From the Department of Justice, Criminal Division," the embossment declares in stern, unyielding font. I do not need an intuitive prowess to understand the basis of this matter or how it could have occurred in the labyrinth of such a group of corporate executives, who routinely flaunt the role of regulatory enforcement and care very little for improprieties rising from conflicts of interest. Regulatory rules to them are but a distant echo and barely acknowledged.

I rise out of my chair. My head down, I pace around the confines of my office with both hands rubbing my forehead to ease the lines of worry etched by months of ethical battles about the contents of the subpoena that awaits my reading. I question myself: *Could I have done more? Could I have been more effective?* My questions assault me as the voice of my mother, full of acrimony and doubt: *You are the chief ethics officer. A subpoena like this is a mark of failure, a badge of disgrace. How could you have let this happen?*

I seek refuge and attempt to take my mind away from the ominous task in front of me. The voice of my mother intrudes, reminding me how once again I fell short of success by not using my "God-given talent." When I was younger these words cut a deep wound that has never healed and still festers like an uncurable ulcer, gnawing at my soul.

I look at the small cut glass candy dish I keep on my desk. It was my grandmother Hazel's cut glass candy dish. I remember when I was a child, it was always the first stop when I visited her house. She made sure it was always brimming with Brach's ribbon candies, a sweet constant in a world of bitter expectations. It reminds me how her house was my sanctuary as a teenager, the place I fled to escape the suffocating intensity of my mother.

Hazel lived a life full of grace with a pleasant dottiness. It was an authentic life filled with joy and without concern for the past or the future. She served me hot dogs and french fries on Dixie paper plates and Coca-Cola in "reused" red Solo cups. She had a bread box full of Hostess chocolate cupcakes bought from the thrift shop, just for me. On special occasions Hazel invited me to Bojangles. She would always take a Ziploc bag of cut cantaloupe in her purse to eat with Bojangles's sausage gravy.

I remember the day she strangled a snake with her bare hands while talking on the phone with her preacher. When the call ended, she ended the snake's life by beating every square inch of its body with a hammer. Another fond memory are her stories about how her mother raised gamecocks and sold them to people as far away as South America, a testament to a lineage steeped in grit.

Everything Hazel did I found fun and intriguing.

My mother thought everyone on her side of the family, including Hazel, was crazy.

Today, looking at the subpoena, I long to escape this tangled web of family dynamics and the hopeless burdens of my job. Still, a message arrives from Clare, "Did you call your dad? Waiting will only make it worse." I roll my eyes. She knows my perpetual reluctance to engage with my parents. Instead, I always keep our conversations to small talk, never daring to confront them, always deflecting, always agreeing. In the end, I reveal almost nothing, always burying my frustration of my parents and my past deep into my marrow.

I look down again at the subpoena and decide it is the more inviting matter to address. I send Clare another message, "Something has come up here at work that I need to take care of."

She responds, "OK, but what about your dad?"

"I'll call him later."

She sends me a reluctant "OK" and then, "Don't forget Katie is having a friend over for dinner tonight."

My shoulders tighten. "The boy who plays high school tennis?"

"Yes, promise me you will behave."

"Don't I always?"

I can see Clare's scrunched face as she types her reply, "Yeah, until someone mentions tennis."

As in my younger days, I swallow my feelings deep into my gut and get to work. I must set aside the thoughts of my father, and this tennis kid, Katie's friend, too. I review every word of the subpoena and contemplate the intent behind the meaning of the structure of each sentence and paragraph. It requests information about Cogniv-Pharma's speaker program, where the company provides an honorarium of several thousand dollars to physicians who speak about the benefits of the company's new dementia and memory loss drug, RemMem, at events attended by other physicians. These events are not only sponsored by Cogniv-Pharma, but they include lavish dinners and wine tastings at high-end restaurants.

The subpoena also requests information on how sales representatives select high prescribers of RemMem to serve as paid speakers at Cogniv-Pharma events promoting RemMem and copies of all emails between sales representatives and speakers.

In addition to questioning how RemMem is marketed, the subpoena requests information from clinical studies about the efficacy of RemMem and any identified side effects, specifically patient complications related to cranial surgeries. Finally, its requests profit reports that the board of directors endorsed and previously provided to federal oversight agencies, as well as all payments made to physicians participating in clinical trials.

It is clear the Department of Justice seeks to tie everything together into a single fraudulent scheme. The more Cogniv-Pharma pays physicians to prescribe the drug RemMem, the more Cogniv-Pharma receives back in payments from Medicare. The worst part is, they're not wrong, which makes the subpoena a doozy.

Still, the lingering thoughts of my mother and father meld together with the conversation I know I'll have to face later. *This is worse than my junior year in high school.* I find myself thinking back to the last time it seemed my entire world was collapsing around me. I was entering my most important year of playing tennis. It was the typical time during the year when a high school athlete's performance could result in scholarship offers from colleges. My parents did not have endless financial resources, and I knew they had already spent thousands of dollars over the years for me to play tennis. As a result, I turned earning a scholarship into a duty I owed to my mother. The burden of this duty was made heavier, because my brother was no longer living at home, leaving all my mother's attention and expectations to fall on me. The pressure eventually became suffocating. No portents, vibes, or even hints prepared me for the way my life began to change at sixteen years old.

I look down at the subpoena in front of me. It brings back the same feelings of uneasiness I felt when I was a high school junior. Similarly, the subpoena provides me no insight of the unearthing questions it will excavate, unraveling family secrets best left buried, much like the past.

When my father heads off before sunrise for his job in Greenville, South Carolina, I am left alone at breakfast with my mother. During the time my brother lived at our house he dominated over everything. Breakfasts before school echoed with his recounting tennis scores from the morning's newspaper. I always remained silent, pondering my own thoughts. Even if I had wished to inject, words failed me. As a result, my mother never recognized my quiet, introspective nature.

Now just the two of us, my mother and I sit in silence at the breakfast table, until my mother begins to cry, "You never talk to me in the morning. Can't you say something like, 'What are you doing today?' I cannot stand it being so quiet."

Empathetic to my mother's wishes, I begin to make small talk and share more about myself during our time together at breakfast. Eventually and without knowing, I begin to swim deep in the emotions and psychology of my mother as our conversations turn to tennis each morning.

Before my junior year in high school, I held the number one position on my high school team as a sophomore and led the team to a third consecutive state championship. Despite this, my year of playing regional Southern Tennis Association tournaments my sophomore year was dismal, and my ranking was precariously low, placing me in the 85–105 group—far from scholarship-worthy.

While my sophomore year of tournament tennis fell short of expectations, I approach the new tournament season of my junior year with revived confidence. At the conclusion of last tournament season, I finished sixth at the year's final tournament, the Southern Indoor Invitational in Louisville, Kentucky.

Unlike my brother, I was not very studious, and my SAT score was horrible. So, I knew my junior year of tennis meant college scholarships hung in the balance, and the one thing I wanted and was determined to achieve by the end of the tennis season was a scholarship off er to the Citadel. My mother, thrilled with the prospect, used our time at breakfast to remind me how proud she would be when she had a son, on a full scholarship no less, at the prestigious military college of South Carolina.

I look down once more at the subpoena. Confidence stirs within me, yet I know the CEO, much like my mother, will seek to impose his will on Cogniv-Pharma's response. Like my mother, his demands will be unreasonable, his tolerance for dissent minimal. He will challenge my many years of legal experience and professionalism.

I tell myself, *Do not back down.*

CHAPTER THREE

Over the last year, I have been advising Cogniv-Pharma executives of the significant regulatory risk associated with the practices executed by the company to market and promote sales of RemMem. The bottom drawer of my desk overflows with memos to the chief executive officer, corporate counsel, and the chairman of the board of directors, marked "Confidential." For years, the Department of Justice has warned physicians and pharmaceutical companies how paid speaking arrangements may act as improper inducements and lead to overprescribing and overuse of a drug based on a physician's loyalty to a company rather than because it is the best treatment for the patient.

I think how much of my life has been affected by the yoke of *loyalty*.

I pore over each memo sitting in my desk drawer, each penned with a personal investment as the guardian of the organization's integrity and reputation. In each memo I remind the board of directors of their pivotal role as the bedrock of Cogniv-Pharma's ethical standing. My intent was clear: to caution capable company leaders against actions that may lack justice and ethics. I underscored the profound and far-reaching impact such decisions could inflict upon our company and the community.

Asserting this fundamental duty, forthrightly and honestly, resulted in an inbox full of cautions from the CEO and general counsel expressing their doubt. "You should be careful with your opinions,"

"These are strong opinions," or, "Other companies are doing the same thing. We all can't be wrong, can we?"

Stress rises and pools into my fingertips. I glance at the candy dish on my desk. It is empty, uninviting, unlike Hazel's when it once was always full of candies. Doubt gnaws at me, but I have no choice other than to begin typing a memo to the chief executive officer, Mr. Graves, explaining the implications of the subpoena for Cogniv-Pharma. I know what to say, but the anticipated skepticism weighs heavily on me. Speaking up has never been my strong suit, a struggle ingrained since childhood, throughout my days of playing tennis, and even today.

I begin typing the memo. Like my tennis strokes, my words flow effortlessly as I describe the legal nuances and the regulatory risks each presents. But when I approach the section where I anticipate conflict with the CEO's expectations, doubt creeps in. Driven by his unyielding pursuit of success, he echoes my mother's same criticisms. Rather than words, typos mar the page as I labor at deleting and retyping.

The computer screen fades in and out, and I see the CEO's intimidating stare, his chiseled chin held high in an assertion of his superiority. Beside him, I see my mother sitting by the tennis court with her crossed arms and jaw clenched, silently admonishing me, "You're not trying your best."

The memory of my mother's disapproving stare grips me like a constrictor. Beside me, I see the legal pad on which I have been scribbling notes. Frustrated, I slam it on my desk with the same disdain and disgust I demonstrated during the opening tournament of my junior year, when I slammed my racket onto the court.

The opening tennis tournament of my junior year began in April. The first tournament was in Aiken, South Carolina, and happened to occur on my birthday. Although I spent the winter months, against my mother's wishes, playing recreation league basketball, I felt a few weeks of practice on the tennis court in late March was enough to shake off any rust and begin climbing the hill to achieve a ranking at the end of the year worthy of a scholarship to the Citadel.

For my first match I am paired against a less experienced and unranked player. He is small, at least six inches shorter, and his oversized racket appears larger than his torso. My opponent is a "pusher," and his nickname is Booker the Pusher. He never attempts to hit a winner. Instead, from the first point of the match, he does nothing more than chase down every shot I hit and return it using only my pace.

His defensive style of play exacerbates my lack of practice time and preparation. He neutralizes me, especially with his high lobs, which provide him with time to never be out of position for my next shot.

I hit every first serve hard and deep into the service box, but all he does is stick his oversized racket out and the ball comes back over the net. I torque my forehand to maximize topspin. The same result.

I am down in the first set and try to mediate my festering rage. I am close to meltdown when my lack of preparation shows its worst. Impatient, I begin a streak of unforced errors, forehands into the net, double faults, and wild backhands that spray all over the court.

I see my mother sitting by the tennis court with her crossed arms and jaw clenched. Her posture sends me the message, "You're not trying your best."

I try a new strategy by attacking the net. I hit a perfect slice backhand approach shot. It stays low and deep as I rush the net. Again, another lob and I set myself up for an overhead winner but hit the ball off the frame and high into the air past the baseline.

I lose the first set 2–6. I see my mother sitting by the tennis court with her arms still crossed and jaw still clenched. I look at her and say to myself, *I cannot believe I am losing to this little pissant.*

Choking is the only way to describe how I played during the second set. My body knows and prepares itself for trouble. My arms and legs freeze up. I look again to the side. My mother is walking to the car, leaning forward with her fist clenched. She turns, blows me a kiss, and says in an absurd, intentional, sappy voice, "Happy birthday, precious!"

Angry and nervous at the same time, I play not to lose. I am right where my opponent wants me. I beat myself in the second set, 3–6. After the last point I slam my racket against the court causing it to fold like a piece of paper.

I enter the car and my mother wails at me, "I should have never allowed you to play basketball."

Because being compliant to my mother is my self-taught method of survival, I hang my head and only reply, "You are right."

My mother cries the entire one-hour drive home. I sit in the third seat of the Buick. We do not speak until my mother crosses the bridge going into our neighborhood and I ask, "Mom, can you let me out at the pond?"

I walk out of my office, slamming the door upon my exit. I walk to the break room, seething. I sit with a bottle of water and try to collect myself. As I sit in silence, semiconsciously reading the bulletin board material in the break room, my heart finally intervenes. I need a break and Lake Mirror, which sits just outside of my office, offers a calm escape.

Walking around the scenic two-mile circle, I feel a moment of catharsis as the natural world unfolds her harmonies before me. I am no longer overwhelmed by the task in front of me. I become conscious of my place as the sun warms my face. In the distance, a fish jumps as if to greet me with a wave of its tail fin. A frog jumps from a lily pad into the water. It comes up again. His eyes just above the rippling water line, he gives me an unblinking stare. Turtles sitting on a log, lined up in order of size, gaze at a bright pink roseate spoonbill wading in the shallow water.

The gentle bonds of nature, like an oriental balm, soothe my ragged mind as I circle by Hollis Gardens. The sweet perfumes waft and hold me as I admire the garden's neoclassical design. I enter the garden for a moment and sit in the cool mist of the moist grotto, where the limestone walls drip with cool water from an artesian well. I take off my shoes and socks and enjoy the cool granite floor, a sensation that is both relaxing and invigorating. The moment refreshes my spirit, and I return to my office, walking past the majestical fountain shaped like a swan and circulating water into Lake Mirror. Nature has always given this sense of peace to me.

Rejuvenated, when I returned to the office, I finish the memo and review it, comparing my response to the information contained in the subpoena. I have accounted for everything except one matter: *any identified side effects, specifically patient complications related to cranial surgeries.* Unfamiliar with whether or not studies of RemMem document any side effects or patient complications related to cranial surgeries, I seek the aid of Dr. Pong.

As the chief medical officer for Cogniv-Pharma, Dr. Pong carries himself with the posture of a soldier who has dedicated his entire life and sacrificed his time with his family to saving and improving the lives of others. Personally, I cherish Dr. Pong's intellectual steadiness, never rushing to an opinion and always basing his conclusions on clinical evidence from peer-reviewed literature. He has never sought the grand stage, but, instead, has preferred to be a majestic shadow ensuring each new drug has proved its worth and, more importantly, caused no harm.

Often, Dr. Pong has been someone I look to be the "calm" in my own personal storms. He knows the value of words and how they can soothe the soul like the gentle flow of a cool river on a hot day.

I arrive at Dr. Pong's office. It sits empty and dark. I wait. Fidgety, I begin to pace as my mind braces for the potential impact of what I may discover.

After fifteen minutes, impatience overcomes me. I leave his office and take the elevator to the basement, home to the organization's medical library. There, among the high, dusty shelves, sit years of medical publications. Also within the grimy, moldy stacks is each clinical research study involving a physician engaged by Cogniv-Pharma.

When I walk into the basement library the damp air and the musty smell of mold engulf me. I scratch my eyes and hear someone from behind a set of stacks slowing turning pages. I look around the corner and find Dr. Pong leaning his body on a shelf and furiously reading. His back is turned to me, but from his posture and rapid pace I detect his concern.

I clear my throat and say, "Dr. Pong." He turns around.

"Good morning, John. What brings you down here?" His dry humor sparks the hint of a smirk as he continues, "Looking for some light reading?"

I reply with raised eyebrows, "I wish. I'm actually looking for you." I hold up the subpoena for him to see and say, "I need some help with this."

"What's that? From the looks of the formality, it does not look good."

I show Dr. Pong the subpoena and, following my finger, we read together, "any identified side effects, specifically patient complications related to cranial surgeries."

Dr. Pong looks up at me and asks, "Is this about RemMem?"

"Yes."

"Well, this is interesting."

"Do you know if any of the many studies conducted on RemMem included any mention or observations of any identified side effects, specifically side effects related to patient complications related to cranial surgeries?"

"No," replies Dr. Pong. He scratches his head and says, "But RemMem is why I am down here."

"What do you mean?"

"John, you are our chief ethics officer so I know you will keep this in confidence. Over the past three weeks I have received phone calls from a few neurosurgeons across the country. Each recently operated on a patient who had been taking RemMem. The patients tolerated the surgery. However, each patient had postsurgical complications and unfortunately did not survive."

"Oh goodness."

Dr. Pong's words are like a punch to the gut.

"Yes, that's why I am down here. I am reviewing some of the studies that were submitted as part of the FDA approval process. So far, none of the physician investigators of the studies I have reviewed have noted such complications."

"That's good, but do you think there is a problem? I mean obviously there must be if the Department of Justice is asking for information about side effects."

Dr. Pong, always conservative with his conclusions until he is confident in the evidence, replies, "So far, the calls I have received are far from being a significant sample. Plus, I want to review all the studies."

Dr. Pong shows me his list of physicians who took part in clinical studies of RemMem as principal investigators. When I look at his list, I instantly see many of the same names that appear on the subpoena. My stomach sinks. I point to the physician names on the subpoena and ask, "Have you reviewed any of these physicians yet?"

Dr. Pong replies, "Yes. Just a few. Interestingly, the physicians listed in the subpoena you are holding appear to have significantly more patients in their studies than the physicians not named in the subpoena." He lowers his legal pad where he has been writing notes and I see the numbers beside each physician.

"What about side effects or postsurgical problems? Have you found anything?"

"So far, none of the studies I have examined have any documented side effects, complications, or significant adverse outcomes. And certainly nothing about complications related to cranial surgeries, so I am not jumping to any conclusions."

I consider Dr. Pong's words and reply, "OK, I will wait to hear more, but for now I will just gather the information requested in the subpoena."

I return to my office and mull over my interaction with Dr. Pong. Although inconclusive, it gives me confidence that Cogniv-Pharma must approach this subpoena with a high regard of seriousness and caution. This eases the grip which had earlier restricted me. I finish the memo and email it to Mr. Graves.

Now, all that remains is to wait.

CHAPTER FOUR

Minutes after I email the memo, Mr. Graves, an accountant and a demigod of calculus, summons me to his office. Tall and imposing, he resides in a plastic universe of accepted symbols and figures. Cold and unforgiving, he views the world as an algorithm void of emotion and human experience, one where everything is mathematically predictive. His attire, immaculate white shirts and custom-made suits, reflects his fastidious nature. He demands the executive team do the same. They all comply, including me.

Mr. Graves, ever consumed by the bottom line, spends his days stalking his next strategic move to seize market share over competing companies, even if it means compromising Cogniv-Pharma's mission to improve health. Alleviating suffering, offering affordable prices, improving patient lives—these he delegates to others, deeming them "necessary overhead expenses." His sole drive is money and power.

As I stand at the meeting table in his office, awaiting his signal to sit, I see my memo in the center. Mr. Graves rises from his desk, pulls back his shoulders and, in his booming voice, says, "Take a seat, John." I take my place, and he joins me across the table. My mind spins with thousands of possibilities. I remind myself to slow down: do not stammer, do not make a mistake, and most of all don't back down.

Mr. Graves looks down at the memo with his cold blue eyes, raises his sharp chin, and says, "John, what is this? I thought all this compliance stuff had been taken care of?"

"Yes, sir," I respond. Suddenly numb terror creeps throughout my body, a feeling all too familiar from my days of playing tennis. Despite my efforts, my voice begins to fail. I struggle to continue, saying, "I evaluated the compliance risks associated with these practices and during the time of their implementation shared them many times." I avoid saying, "with you," to prevent direct conflict. I learned this at an early age, and it is etched into my consciousness.

Mr. Graves thrusts his jaw forward. "Compliance risks? There is nothing wrong with what we are doing. It's just goddamn smart business. Don't you understand that?"

Vulnerability rises through my spine. I take a slow breath. "Yes, but now the federal government is involved and is seeking information about our marketing practices—"

"Just stop right there." Worry grabs my chest when Mr. Graves interrupts me. "Your job is to keep the government and all these money-hungry attorneys as far away from me as possible. As I see it, the memo you just emailed to me fucking agrees with them. As a matter of fact, your memo is an embarrassment. It is nothing but a reiteration of what the Department of Justice is stating."

Feeling imprisoned, I immediately accept defeat and maneuver my mind into self-preservation mode. As in dealing with my mother, compliance and false dedication become my shield and protect me from the insurmountable task confronting me.

Mr. Graves continues, "Now listen to me closely. You will stay out of this matter. Our general counsel will fix your problem, and you can sign off on it if you like. Understood?"

"Yes, sir."

I momentarily think back to my mother.

"You will never play recreation league basketball again, understood?"

"Yes, ma'am."

"This is the end, understood?"

"Yes, ma'am."

Mr. Graves continues, "Do you not see that if we do not engage physicians and pay them to support our product, we won't sell a damn thing and will have to sell our corporation to a competitor and, by God, I will not allow that."

"Yes, sir."

Again, I think back to my mother.

"Do you not see how I know what is best for you?"

"Yes, ma'am."

My silence in front of Mr. Graves tells him I have nothing more to share.

"Now, do you have any questions?"

I give a reluctant pause. His question is rhetorical. I have heard such rhetorical questions my entire life; however, I must ask, "What about the upcoming board of directors meeting?" I open my hands to invite a peaceable reply: "An ethics update is on the agenda."

Mr. Graves thinks for a moment, staring at the ceiling. "There is no reason to take your update off the agenda. Now, get on with your day. I will update the chairman and take care of this for now."

I walk out of Mr. Graves's office. Over the last two years he has fired four executives who questioned his leadership or his decisions. *Am I next?*

I expect by the end of the day to receive the same fate. I think to myself, *My family cannot afford it.*

My frugal parents made do by rarely staying in hotels when we traveled to tennis tournaments. They stretched their money thin, enabling me to compete in more tournaments. This meant waking up before sunrise and sleeping in the back of the Buick Estate with its back seats folded down—the fabric's hard, scratchy surface was always a skin irritant. Sometimes I could fall asleep, but I still felt every bump on the road and every turn along the way. It was not until my junior year that we began to stay at hotels.

The humiliation of Aiken motivates me at the next tournament, which is at the Florence Country Club. After I breeze through my first match, my mother drives us over to the Days Inn. The sun sits high in the sky, but still the halogen sign of the Days Inn buzzes like a glowing bug zapper.

After my mother checks in, she drives us around the hotel as we count room numbers, looking for our room. Finding it, she backs the Buick into the space at the door. I jump out of the car, throw my tennis bags on my bed, and skip over to check out the pool. There is not much to see, but I am happy the water in the small cement rectangle is clear and there is a diving board.

Excited for a swim to cool down, I run back to our room and change. When I arrive, my mother struggles to bring in the cooler of frozen food, with its seasoned meat for tacos, which she will reheat on a hot plate for dinner in the room. Still, she does not say anything as I slip by her and rush to the bathroom to change.

The next day, I win both of my matches. In the evening, as I head for the pool, my mother plugs in her toaster oven and heats leftover pizza she has brought from home. After the pool, we prop up in our respective beds, eat pizza, and watch TV. My mother says, "John, if you win your semifinal match tomorrow, we will have to stay another night."

I shrug my shoulders and reply, "So."

My mother turns at me and smiles. "Well, because we are out of all the food I packed, we will need to go out to eat."

My opponent in the semifinals is someone who beat me the year before in high school matches. We had never played against each other in Southern Tennis Association tournaments. Despite the sometimes-ridiculous pressure I feel from my mother, the burden I place on my shoulders for this match is fueled by my hatred of losing twice in a row to the same person.

My mother had not been at our previous match, so, unlike my high school teammates, she does not know my opponent's father owned Krispy Kreme franchises. As in our previous match, my opponent's father arrives, clad in his distinctive Krispy Kreme green pants and matching green polo shirt, adorned with its characteristic "bow-tie"-like emblem, all topped off with a Krispy Kreme ball cap.

I do quick work on the court and revenge my earlier three-set loss with a 6–2, 6–2 win. As we walk together back to the car my mother says, "I am glad that was fast. Watching his father made me hungry. I am dying for a donut."

We do not visit Krispy Kreme. Instead, my mother drives us to dinner at Wendy's, which includes a Frosty to go.

The next morning, the screaming whirring of my mother's hair dryer awakens me. The match is scheduled for 9:00. It is just 7:00 and my mother prepares herself for the day. My mother's buzzing hair dryer heats up the small hotel room. The sound coupled with the heat irritates me. Annoyed, I roll over and try to go back to sleep. Unsuccessful, I snap at my mom, "Are you about finished?"

She shuts it off and turns toward me. "You must be nervous about today. You just need to be tough like your brother."

I will never attain this standard set by my mother, and she will never understand.

In the finals, I face the number one player in the state, a formidable opponent I have never beaten. Gossip swirls around the court that he plans to forgo his college scholarships and turn pro after high school. I am still waiting for my first scholarship offer.

My mother hears this and says to me, "I don't care what they say. You have more talent than him. If you put it all together you can beat him."

I appreciate my mother's comment, but I have no idea what it means to "put it all together."

At the beginning of the match, I win an early service break to go up 1–0. My serve consistently overpowers my opponent, so I do not worry about breaking his serve a second time. I win each of my service games and take the first set, 6–4.

After winning the first set, I feel my arms and legs tense, but my serve continues to keep me steady, and the second set is tied at 3–3.

Long rallies fill the next game. I do not attack but stay at the baseline and we trade powerful ground strokes torqued with topspin. We exchange deuce scores several times when I have a break point. I surprise my opponent by charging the net after my service return. He manages to whip his racket around and fires a passing shot past me. I see it sail just beyond the baseline and call it out. I am up 4–3 and ready to complete an extraordinary victory, when my opponent looks at his mom and walks off the court to ask for a line judge.

Junior tennis is the only sport in which players are expected to call their own lines. All other sports have adults serving as umpires or referees to make judgment calls and keep score. But the virtual absence of such umpires in junior tennis makes cheating prevalent, as well as gamesmanship.

I know the ball was out and my call was correct. However, my nerves surge as I watch my opponent return to the court with a charming senior citizen to serve as line judge. My opponent and I had not exchanged heated words, and our match had been civil. However, as the line judge introduces herself with a lecture on court ethics and fairness, I begin to fall apart.

Seeing this, once the match resumes, my opponent begins questioning every call I make, even if it is obvious. I lose the next eight points. Suddenly, the second set goes from a sure victory in my favor to my opponent serving to win the second set.

Doubt rises from the pit of my stomach. At the same time, I constantly question the fairness of my new situation, as I battle not only my opponent, but also the rising heat of the morning.

My mother begins clapping after each point and yelling out words of encouragement that bluntly embarrass me. After losing the next game, I walk to the net to shake my opponent's hand. I did not realize I had lost track of the score and did not realize the score was still just 5–4. Nevertheless, my opponent shakes my hand, and we depart the court.

My mother does not say anything until we are both in the car. She shouts at me, "You realize your match was not over?"

I furrow my brow and reply, "What do you mean?"

"It was only 5–4 when you walked off the court. I tried to tell you this, but you never listened to me."

"Oh," I respond in surprised confusion.

"You never finished the match! How could you have lost count of the score? I cannot believe we drove all the way to Florence, spent money to stay in a hotel, and you lose by forgetting the score."

"But why didn't the line judge say something?" I plead.

"That old fart? Don't you have enough sense to know she was just there to call the lines?" My mother hits her hand on the steering wheel and continues, "Also, do you know how many times you played balls that were out, just because he got that damn line judge?"

I soak up my mother's emotions like a sponge. Her anxiety and disappointment seep into me, mingling with thoughts of my defeat on the court and the money my parents spent on the weekend.

The ride home is long and filled with sarcastic comments like, "That was an expensive way to spend a weekend so you could enjoy a swimming pool." I shut down and just stare out the windshield.

I spend the remainder of the day in my office, waiting. My stomach, a large, knotted ball, refuses to untangle no matter how much I try to distract myself with other work. By the end of the day, nothing changes. I recognize how my innate ability to shut down allows me to endure the moment and preserve my position.

I grab my car keys and go to my car. Still nervous from the day's confrontation, I fumble with my keys as I unlock the door. In the car I feel safe, removed from the stress of work. I take a deep breath, finding solace, only to realize the stress of the office caused me to forget about my father's earlier phone call. *I will deal with my father later.*

I grow more relaxed, settled in, and start home. But my respite is short-lived. While I'm driving home, my father calls again. I breathe deeply, set my mind to autopilot, and answer the call.

"John, this is your father. What have you been up to?"

This is his usual greeting, and I hold back my immediate exasperation and urge to say something obnoxious. Instead, I say in a plainspoken tone, "Dad, I've been working."

Without hesitation my father replies in his usual disconnected and abrupt tone, "Listen, John, I need to talk with you." I notice my father's voice getting shaky. This is unusual. He continues, "It's about your mother. I am taking her to the doctor tomorrow. She is not doing well."

I know why he is taking her to the doctor and feel a sense of relief; however, I still follow up with questions. My mother has always been domineering so asking my father questions allows him to feel in control and that he is making all the decisions. "Is everything OK?" I reply.

My father's voice changes into one of monotone restraint. "John, your mother's memory, it's getting worse. I am having a hard time managing her." He pauses and repeats, "A really hard time."

This feels like an extension of my day and I'm hesitant to talk about it, though Clare has been pushing me to have a candid discussion with my father. My nerves are still on edge from the interaction with Mr. Graves, but there's little I can do to avoid the conversation my father clearly wants to have.

"What do you mean it's gotten worse?"

"Well, it just has. She is repeating herself more and she is forgetting things. She lost her sudoku book yesterday. Not only did she accuse me of hiding it from her, but she threw a tirade and yelled at me for about thirty minutes."

My mother has always pointed fingers at my father whenever something went missing, or house or yard projects did not go as planned. I cannot recall a time when my father was not the target or scapegoat of her accusations. I remain silent in response to my father, recognizing how my mother habitually blames him for even the smallest unintentional mishap.

Yet, amid her accusations, I sense a profound mystery surrounding my mother. There appears an elusive depth to her that I can feel, but not grasp—a secrecy she guards closely, especially her past, which she never shares with anyone.

I recall the first time I felt this mystery was when Hazel stopped by our house on the way home from an Amway tour. In the back of her long tan Oldsmobile sat a boxed grandfather clock needing assembly and she asked my father and me to put it together for her.

After Hazel leaves, my mother examines the box. Wrinkling her face at the picture on its side she hollers, "I do not know what is more embarrassing. The fact that my mother went on an Amway tour, or that she wants to place this cheap-ass clock in her living room."

Together, my father and I spend hours separating the particleboard panels, screws, and plastic weights and chains. Nearly finished, we discover a certain piece of particleboard lacks the required pre-drilled holes. With a drill, we attempt to rectify this oversight by boring two holes, but the fragile nature of the particleboard causes it to splinter, cracking the plastic veneer and leaving an unsightly blemish. We realize our mistake: not only drilling the holes, but how we had the wrong piece of wood.

We finish assembling the clock and my mother comes up to inspect it. She looks it over and asks, "What happened here?" pointing at where my father and I drilled the holes. We explain our mistake and my mother bursts into tears. "You two are so thoughtless. I cannot believe you ruined Mother's clock."

My father replies, "But you know as well as I do how cheap this thing is. After all, it's from an Amway tour."

My mother, still crying, goes to her bedroom exclaiming, "That does not matter. It's my mother's and you ruined it!"

Still on the phone, my father continues, "She can sit and finish these sudoku puzzles, but she cannot remember where she put her glasses or cannot find her coffee cup in the mornings. When I hint that maybe she is forgetting things she yells, 'How the hell could I do these puzzles if something was wrong?' If I tell her she is repeating herself she blows up and tells me she is not going crazy like the rest of her family."

My mother's memory is slipping away, a slow and heartbreaking decline. Her once clear world now grows opaque and dim. Words vanish midway through sentences, items are misplaced without recollection, and even recent interactions with friends and neighbors slip from her mind. She dismisses these lapses with a reticent remark, saying, "I must be going crazy like the rest of my family," believing her side of the family to be plagued by madness and insanity.

As my father talks on, the images effortlessly flood my mind. I see my mother sitting in the orange leather chair in the den—a piece of furniture I have always thought was the ugliest, most uncomfortable chair in the house. However, it has been a treasure of hers since before I was born.

All day, she divides her time between sitting in the orange leather chair, working sudoku puzzles, and sitting at the breakfast room table, looking out the back window and commenting on the neighbors walking on the road that backs up to the yard.

Thinking of the breakfast room window gives me a cold shiver. As a child my seat at the breakfast room table was at the back, against the window. My parents on both sides and my older brother in front of me. Like everything in our house, even family meals could escalate into confusion and anger. Every day I had to eat each meal anticipating the level of intensity, knowing I had no way to escape to a more peaceful place.

My memory fades as my father pauses briefly, giving me an opportunity to ask, "Dad, which doctor are you taking Mom to see?"

"Dr. Knuckles."

"Have you considered taking Mom to a neurologist? Dr. Knuckles is her primary care doctor."

"John, we have been seeing him for fifteen years and your mother likes him. Anyway, a neurologist would probably cost a fortune."

Irritation begins to fester. "Dad, you have insurance. Stop being cheap. Also, have you ever thought how Mom knows Dr. Knuckles and exactly what to say to hide her memory loss?"

He quickly interjects: "Just let me handle your mother. I know what she needs."

I sense the conversation closing and take the opportunity to ask about the elephant in the room: "Dad, how's Mom's drinking?"

For several years, my mother has been living with back pain. White wine relieves her pain. The same white wine allows her to dismiss the reality that she is losing her memory as, each day, a few of the tiny capillaries filling her head with blood slowly burst and dry, leaving her brain to atrophy.

I hear his regret before he even speaks. After a long pause he says, "Son, she drinks a little throughout the day, but I can manage it for her."

"OK, make sure you share that with her doctor." A rhetorical statement, because I doubt my father has ever shared his concerns about my mother's drinking and I know she never will. That's what my family has always done, bury their heads in the sand for the sake of pride. I know this information will never be shared with my mother's doctor.

At the same time, it's hard not to think of Dr. Pong and all the studies down in the library and to wonder what pertinent information has not been shared, or even worse, intentionally hidden.

My father's only reply is, "Well, I guess I better let you go now. I will call you tomorrow. Be careful."

"Be careful." My father's standard goodbye, yet I have never been reckless.

When the call ends, I think how my whole life my mother has spoken about her family as if they were lunatics, never mind her claim about how most of the men were just drunks. One crazy cousin was Walter, a preacher who went around town telling people he was close to understanding Jesus. My mother would laugh at him, a radio preacher, when she heard him on the airwaves. "He's just as goofy as the rest of my family."

The sun goes down and I feel the heaviness of twilight when I arrive home. The conflict of the day weighs on my heart. I drive the car into the cul-de-sac and stare a moment at our house. The windows glow with life. I pause. *I am lucky to still have a job.*

I go inside. My tension immediately vanishes when I hear Vivian, my thirteen-year-old daughter say, "Daddy, you're home. Why were you working late?"

I reply, "I wasn't working. I was out with my girlfriend. Your mom is getting a little too old for me. I'm testing out newer, faster models."

Vivian, thirteen and already too familiar with my sarcasm, replies, "Real funny, Dad. I don't know what Mom sees in you, anyway."

"I'll tell you what she sees. She is overly attracted to my intellectual prowess."

Vivian laughs, "You mean she likes nerds who read boring books and take naps every day?"

I stop and examine Vivian. She, like our twin sixteen-year-old daughters, has turned into an adult overnight. I lean over to Vivian and change my voice to a low and salty tone in an attempt to create a more serious complexion, "Let me tell you about the passion I elicit from your mother with this mind and body." I raise my eyebrow and place both hands on my belly.

Vivian yells, "Ewww, Dad! You are gross. Mom, make Dad stop."

Vivian and I laugh as my wife, Clare, walks into the den. She has heard the interaction, as have the twins, who chime in with, "Mom, you are the only adult in the house. Dad's like having another child."

Clare gives me a kiss on the cheek, and I continue my sarcasm and ask, "How's my favorite wife? How was your day as a nurse?" She understands my silliness and how it is a deflection of reality.

"Fine," she replies.

I look back at Vivian and say, "Anyone can be a nurse. All you do is what the doctor tells you." I pause because no one reacts. Then I say, "Of course, your mom is terrible at following directions."

Clare pulls back and gives me a playful, disgusted look. I see her lips curling in a smile. She knows me like a book she's read many times before. Even the parts I'm ashamed of, which are like my mother. She says, "You are quite a comedian this evening. Interesting day?"

I stop my antics and relax. "Ugh, I don't know which is worse, work or my mother."

Clare and I walk to the kitchen. I lean on the kitchen island as she pours me a glass of wine. I take a sip and begin to relax. "Thanks. I needed this." Clare knows about my struggles at work. Telling her about my workday will only worry her more, and I don't want to do that. She takes on enough.

Instead, I ask, "Is Henry home from football practice?" Henry is our high school senior who has played football for the past four years. Named after my paternal grandfather, Henry, like him he is a sports fanatic, especially when it comes to football.

Clare immediately senses my diversion and says, "Yes, but let's talk about your day and why your dad called."

I take a deep breath and begin. "So, Dad claims he is taking Mom to the doctor tomorrow."

"That's good. I cannot believe she is actually going. How did he convince her?"

"I don't know. Maybe he plans to hog-tie her? Maybe sedate her? Who knows? I am just glad she is going."

"Yes, me, too," Clare replies. "I just hope they are prepared for what they may hear."

I take a long swallow. "I guess we will know soon enough."

Dinner is a cheerful time. We sit around the dining room table and Katie's friend, Joe, joins us, sitting by Katie. I raise an eyebrow when I see them holding hands at the table. Katie sees me and pulls her hand away. Still uncomfortable with the situation, she attempts a conversation, saying, "Dad, did you know Joe plays tennis on the high school team?" I do not reply, so she continues, "This is Joe's first year on the team. Tell him about how you played on the high school team."

Avoiding the subject I reply, "That's good," and continue eating.

Katie gives a stare of discontent to Clare, which coaxes her to say, "John, Katie would like for you to share about your high school days playing tennis."

I look down at my watch and then at Joe. I say, "So, Joe, you play on the high school team."

"Yes, sir."

I rub my palms during the moment of awkward silence. "Do you enjoy it?"

"Yes, sir."

"Good," I reply, "I am glad. That is important." I go back to my meal.

"Daaad," whines Katie, "Can you share a little more? This is Joe's first year on the high school team."

I take a deep breath and say, "Katie, I am sure rather than have me bore everyone with stories about my days of playing tennis, you and Joe would rather go see a movie or do something."

Henry, now home from football practice, chimes in, "Yeah, especially since Dad did not play a real sport like football."

I give Henry my "but I am still strong and young enough to kick your ass" look.

Katie has tried before, and she knows this is going nowhere. She replies, "Can we have some money for the movie?"

"Sure," I hand her a fifty-dollar bill and say, "and I expect some change."

The meal is over, and Clare and I clear the table and take the dishes to the kitchen sink. In the kitchen Clare's look of disdain is obvious. "John, you know some day your money and jokes are going to run out. Then what are you going to do when the kids ask about tennis?"

I say, "Oh, hell, Clare, I don't know," and walk into the den and turn on a rerun of *Everybody Loves Raymond*. Mary is on the couch. I look at her, but before I can say anything she says, "Yes, Dad. I know. This is show is exactly how our life would be if we lived across the street from your parents."

Then she catches me by surprise and asks, "Dad, I heard you and Mom in the kitchen. Why don't you ever talk about when you played tennis?"

"I dunno, I just don't like talking about it."

"Did something bad happen?"

"Not really, sweetheart. It's just a part of my past I would rather forget."

C H A P T E R   F I V E

The next morning, like a thief, the unforgiving buzz of my iPhone steals my slumber. Mr. Graves fills my inbox. "You are scheduled to brief the board chairman in the coming days? I need to see what you plan to share with him by the end of the day."

I feel suffocated. My muscles grow tight and twist beneath my skin. My mind and my heart diverge sharply. My mind, practical and disciplined, understands the value of perseverance and the necessity of employment. Meanwhile, my heart, passionate and at times rebellious, yearns for truth and cries for freedom.

I roll out of the bed. Clare looks over at me and asks in a sleepy voice, "Why are you getting up so early?"

"My boss does not have a life other than work and he expects me to have the same."

She rolls over and continues, "I thought maybe it was your dad."

As I feel around the nightstand for my eyeglasses, I reply, "It really does not matter. Neither one of them listen to a damn thing I have to say."

I go downstairs. Our two dogs, a black Labrador and a much older beagle, welcome me by thumping their tails against the chest in the hallway. I let them out for their morning business and fill their food bowls as the herbal, smoky aroma of brewing coffee begins to float through the kitchen and awaken my senses.

I open the back door and the black Lab, Hazel, sprints to her bowl. She finishes her morning meal before the ten-year-old beagle, Hoke, returns from the backyard.

I take a mug of coffee to the back porch along with my laptop. A low-hanging moon looms large. It commands my attention with its stoic grace enhanced by an ethereal white halo. Tree frogs sing their final chorus of nocturnal tunes, while down by the lake a bullfrog, like a tuba, releases a deep croak.

In the distance, I hear the baritone hooting of barred owls, messengers of the divine and a symbol for making peace within broken relationships, calling out, *Who cooks for you? Who cooks for you-all?*

My backyard is a place of intimacy where I feel its presence and it feels mine. It reminds me of my true self. Though I never travel to exotic faraway places, my backyard has always offered a sense of exploration. It is a realm of unencumbered expectations, just like the pond in the neighborhood when I was young. Like the pond, here I find a place where space and time blur, where past and present merge, allowing me to release my emotions without restraint—amid the demands from Mr. Graves, and the lingering memory of the phone call with my father.

As the sun rises, the chirping of the early morning songbirds brings me back to the present, as silhouettes begin to disappear. I savor the fragrant scent of the creamy-white blossoms of the magnolia tree the sun now illuminates.

Magnolia trees, "living fossils," exist as one of the oldest plants on earth, dating back to a time before bees roamed the trees' expansive flowering saucers. I think how the magnolia has adapted over years of evolving changes and cataclysmic events. *I, too, have evolved, or have I?*

The morning haze evaporates, and the rising temperature reminds me of the awaiting workday. I type a few more pages and decide to get a coffee refill. Inside, Clare sits reading a book with her coffee. She smiles and says, "Good morning. You were up early. You got a busy day ahead of you?"

I glance out at the yard, and then turn to Clare. Despite my reluctance to burden her, I am certain she senses my mounting frustration. Besides, there is no way she will not notice now, not with Mr. Graves rousing me at all hours to deal with the mess I tried to warn him about months ago. So, I blurt out, "The company got served with a federal subpoena yesterday. It involves the new drug RemMem."

Clare lifts her head from her book. "Oh! How did that go over?"

"Not good," I say raising my eyebrows. "I tried to get ahead of things in hopes of calming the waters by sending a memo about it to Mr. Graves. That completely backfired."

"Backfired? What do you mean?"

I throw my arms up. "He basically accused me of siding with the government. He told me how my memo was an embarrassment and wants me to stay out of it. He says the general counsel will handle the matter."

"But isn't this a regulatory matter under your scope of practice?"

"Yes, and now the manipulative bastard wants to see what I plan to share with the chairman. The whole thing just pisses me off."

The calm from the backyard slips away from me like a shedding skin. It's not Clare's fault and I regret beginning to lose my temper, which only adds to my frustration.

Clare walks over to refill her coffee. "Well, just be careful."

I cringe and say, "Oh Jesus! You sound like my father. Every time we talk, 'Now, John, be careful.' Do you think I am going to be intentionally reckless? I have lived an entire life of being careful." *Ever since I began to play tennis.*

Clare sighs and relaxes her body. "John, I know it must be difficult how so much is happening at the same time. I know you will do the right thing. You always have. Just remember we are in this together, always."

I relax and place my coffee mug on the counter and approach Clare. I put my arms around her, and she corresponds with hers as I reply, "I know. That is what makes this so hard. If I was by myself, I could just run away. But with you and the kids I have a lot to take care of. Regardless, I know we are a team, and we will stick together."

We look into each other's eyes, smile, and I say, "I promise I will be careful."

At work in my office, I place my laptop computer on my desk and continue typing the quarterly compliance report to the chairman. After many years of practice, my craft is seasoned and principled. My report, professional and accurate. It explains the subpoena, each questionable act and how each issue addressed in the subpoena potentially implicates the company in acts of regulatory noncompliance. Furthermore, it explains how fully cooperating with the Department of Justice will potentially mitigate the situation and protect the reputation and assets of the company. I make no assumptions and only include the facts.

I take my time writing the update to make sure everything is corroborated by industry literature. Everything I suggest is what good boards and good management do. Still, I second-guess myself before I email it to Mr. Graves.

My second-guessing began when I was younger and playing tennis. I avoided conflict with my mother by saying the things I knew she wanted to hear, even if it meant lying. As a teenager, coping with the stress of schoolwork and relationships plus going to the tennis courts each day to practice or play a match was exhausting. Many times, I played with minimal effort, just wanting to get the match over with and go home and rest. I did not care about winning, and although I lost, when I arrived home and my mother asked, "How did you do?" I lied and replied, "I won."

Avoiding conflict by telling Mr. Graves what he wants to hear is not an option. Unlike in my earlier days of avoiding my mother, I appreciate how my duty has nothing to do with pleasing him. Still, the expected conflict makes me nervous and too much is at stake. *I cannot back down, but I must be careful.*

When I arrive home after work, Clare is setting the dining table for dinner. The dining room is my favorite room in the house. Clare decorated the room with bird prints by Anne Worsham Richardson and a print by Alice Ravenel Huger Smith, each a personal reminder of South Carolina and my longing to be home.

Everyone prepares their plates, and we sit at the table with steaming servings of pasta. The mood is light, but before I can take my first bite my iPhone buzzes. I look down and see an email from Mr. Graves. My day began with him, and it is now ending with him. As I leave the table to read it, I hear Vivian say, "Why is Dad always working?"

I give Clare an uncomfortable glance as if to say, "Sorry." I go into the living room to read the email. It simply says, "Here is your report." The simple sentence feels like a gut punch. I open the attachment and receive a slap in the face. The pieces of the report where I painstakingly highlighted the regulatory risks and the need to cooperate with the Department of Justice have been redacted. I finish reading it and say to myself, *This is meaningless and states nothing more than the company was served with a federal subpoena. What a crock of shit.*

I begin to shake with anger when I read the rewritten portions of the memo. *Our culture of professional ethics ensures Cogniv-Pharma's commitment to regulatory compliance. Therefore, I am certain this matter presents no risk to the company. The Cogniv-Pharma board of directors and management should have no concerns about corporate or personal liability.*

A promise of certainty, just like a religion of certainty, is very dangerous. I think to myself, *I doubt Mr. Graves has forgotten about the numerous memos I wrote to him detailing how the Department of Justice skepticism about pharmaceutical speaker programs and the concern about fraud.* I also was familiar with how Mr. Graves hardly ever gave credence to the concerns I raised. "John, how can it be wrong when every other company is doing the same thing?"

The dining room becomes quiet as everyone picks up on my tension. Someone calls to me, "Is everything OK, Dad?"

I read over the report again. My face hardens. I give a heavy sigh and call back from the living room, "Yes, just hold on a minute. Dad's got to take care of this."

I begin typing on my iPhone, with an attempt at neutrality, "There are a few things within the report that appear to have been removed. Is this correct?"

I receive an almost instant reply: "Yes, I took these out. Not necessary."

Despair rolls across my face as something snaps within me. When this happened on the tennis court, I threw my racket or yelled out in frustration. Here, those are not options, but still I struggle to hold back my mounting frustration and type, "I suggest we either add this back into the report or we footnote the report and state how it has been amended. As the organization's chief ethics officer and because of my direct role with the chairman, intentionally taking this out of the report compromises my duty to the board."

I wait a few minutes. Nothing. The kids call from the dining room, "Dad, are you coming back to the table? The pasta is so delicious." I look down at my iPhone. Still, nothing. I return to the table.

Clare looks up at me. "Is everything OK?"

"No," I reply in a gruff voice. "Mr. Graves is—" Before I finish my iPhone begins to ring. "Goddamn it!" I look down, expecting Mr. Graves. It's not. It is my father. He has always had impeccable timing. I used to feel sorry for him, but now he's in my way, too.

"It's my father. I cannot deal with him right now."

Clare replies, "He may want to talk about your mother. Didn't he take her to the doctor today?"

"Jesus Christ, Clare. Please, I am trying to enjoy dinner. It is hard enough that I must deal with my boss. Now, my dad is calling."

Clare presses her lips. She restrains her impatience with me and says, "You need to hear what your dad has to say."

She's right and I'm embarrassed this happened in front of the kids. I press accept and walk out of the dining room with my iPhone.

"John. This is your father. I took your mother to the doctor today. He thinks she may be losing her memory."

I want to say, *No shit, Dad, tell me something we do not all already know*, but I pause to collect my feelings. Instead, I ask, "What do you think about that?"

"Well, what I don't understand is how she can do all these *suduko* books."

I take a deep breath and say, "I don't know, Dad, but she is clearly repeating herself and obviously forgetting things."

"Well, son, the doctor gave us a prescription for that so I am hoping it will get better."

"Dad," I try to hold my exasperation. "This is not going to get better. The medicine will only slow it down. What did he prescribe?"

"He prescribed…let me see. RemMem. That's the drug your company makes, right?"

"Yes, it is." I begin to think about the subpoena and the conversation I had with Dr. Pong. *What are the odds?* Then I think about how Mom does not need surgery so maybe this is fine. After all, even Dr. Pong had not made a conclusion about surgical complications and there is plenty of evidence the drug does work.

I hear my mother in the background. She yells something at my father I cannot make out, but I can tell she has been drinking, which exacerbates her mood and forgetfulness. "Dad, did you talk to the doctor about her drinking?"

"Son, I have already told you I can manage that for your mom. I bought these three-ounce paper cups—you know the ones people use to rinse their mouth after brushing their teeth?"

I interrupt, "Dad, three-ounce cups are fine, but if she drinks out of them all day long it won't make a difference."

"Son," he says, "just let me handle it." There is a brief pause, and he follows up, saying, "I'll let you go now. Be careful."

I finish the call and see a new email from Mr. Graves pop up. "See me in my office first thing tomorrow."

I shut my eyes and feel life pulling every inch of my body in different directions. I must regain my composure before it is too late, and I cause irrevocable damage. I walk into the living room and over to the piano and begin playing a classical tune I learned as a teenager.

In the dining room I hear Mary say, "Mom, do you want me to ask Dad if he is coming back to the table?"

"No, sweetheart. Let's just let him be for a while."

I continue playing as Clare clears the table. Alone in the living room, I linger at the piano and meander through my old repertoire from my ninth-grade piano recital. When I finish the downstairs is dark. Everyone has gone to bed. I feel more at ease, and my mind is finally clear.

C H A P T E R   S I X

The cardinals, like every morning, are first to sing their morning melodies, lifting them to dawn's first light. I sit at the breakfast room table dressed for work and sip my last cup of coffee to the last bitter drop. At the bird feeder by the window, I watch the male cardinal pick up a seed, hop over to his awaiting female, and delicately place the seed into her beak. Their courtship, a ritual of devotion and adoration, will include building a nest together before living a life of dedicated monogamy. I regret how I treated my family the evening before and promise to do better.

As I watch this tender scene, my mind wonders about the inexplicable and complex dynamic of my parents' relationship. It has not always been one I understood, or understand, but, like the cardinals I am watching, their commitment to one another has always been clear and constant. Now, it has never been more apparent as I witness my father in his advanced age care for my mother and the turbulence of her failing memory. My father's patience, something that always incited my mother's ire, is now a blessing.

Thinking of them, I picture my mother's yard. Rhododendron in the backyard gully grows between the trees, as they do in the North Carolina mountains. Profuse pink and white azaleas burst forth and rival the famous Augusta National plantings, while native Piedmont azaleas exude the sticky sweetness of honeysuckle blooms with their flaming vibrant stamen. Hosta and large autumn fern paint a luscious green background until the first frost.

Everything in my mother's yard has its place. She ensured this. Nothing was planted without her permission. Dad was the only person who could help, but it was under her constant instructions and guidance.

I remember, when I was a boy, my mother never asked for my assistance when working in the yard. I watched her and always asked to help, but her only reply was, "There is really nothing for you to do. But why don't you sit and keep me company." Or she requested, "You can go inside and bring me back some iced tea." Like at work now, regardless of my enthusiasm, I am never asked to perform any significant tasks, until something like the subpoena occurs. However, I know Mr. Graves does not take it seriously and, like my mother, will merely brush me aside like he has already done with my report to the chairman.

Regret tugs at me as I recall the harsh words of the previous evening. I promise myself to do better, to honor the steadfast love that binds my parents and the delicate, enduring dance of the cardinals outside my window that speaks to their commitment.

Dressed in my suit and ready for work, I walk out to the car. I should leave, but the sweet perfume of the vitex tree by the driveway invites me into the backyard. Clare sees me and yells out the back door, "You're going to get your work clothes dirty."

I ignore her warning as my soul retreats into nature, my worries carried off on the gentle breeze as I chase the calm I yearn for and need.

I brush past the blue blooms of the hydrangea; memories of my grandmother's long row of blue hydrangeas sitting in the red dirt beside her house flood my mind. Like her, I find solace in the company of birds and butterflies, ensuring my yard, too, is a haven with a bird feeder filled with sunflower seeds and a tapestry of blooming flowers to attract butterflies and host plants for their eggs and caterpillars.

I continue walking and admire how the hairy stems of the butterfly weed grow. The morning dew has weighted their orange and yellow blooms, making their heads hang down like Jesus on the cross. I peer under the leaves and spot the tiny black monarch eggs. A short row of sea-foam green chrysalises hangs underneath the garden shed, waiting to unfold their transformative beauty. I examine them and contemplate their metamorphosis.

A monarch lands on the butterfly weed. It displays its large, striking orange wings with their distinctive black veins. I ponder the color orange, positive and optimistic, and how the carotenes of orange pigment convert light into energy. Another monarch floats by. It reminds me that orange is also a toxic color that warns of potential dangers.

Inside the chicken coop, Gloria, the large white leghorn hen, calls a warning from the top perch. She, much like my mother, rules the roost with unquestioned authority. Gloria's call reminds me I am now going to be late for work. Not that it matters much—Mr. Graves has made up his mind and my thoughts and presence are unneeded. Still, I continue my saunter over to the bird-of-paradise plants. After two years, their bright orange sepals and blue petals have finally blossomed and I long to admire their exotic splendor once more.

I walk across the grass to the flower bed and rub my eyes in disbelief. Each bird-of-paradise bloom is gone. I stoop down for a closer look. Near the base of each flower and through its waxy green leaves I see how each bloom has been cut. "Damn it," I mutter aloud and begin stomping to the back door.

I throw open the back door. The doorknob hits the side of the washer with a loud metallic bang. I yell, "Vivian, can you please get over here?" I see her begin to move, but she does not move fast enough. "Hurry! I am already late for work."

Vivian rounds the corner into the laundry room. She looks at me with wide blue eyes and says, "Dad, what is all over the bottom of your pants?"

I prepare to speak when the smell hits me. I look down and see dog shit smeared on the hem of my pants and along the sides of my polished leather shoes. My anger is back, hot and boiling in my face. I growl through clinched teeth, "Un-freaking-believable! Of all days!"

Vivian instinctively slips out of my line of sight as I slam the door. In my fury I stop and realize her bewildered face looked just like mine as a child when my mother yelled at me. I remember the look as the unsettling feelings of the past rise in my throat.

I recall the rhododendron bush beside the driveway where my brother and I played basketball, each game more competitive than the last and resulting in broken branches, despite our efforts to avoid it. Each time we snapped a branch, we attempted to hide our destruction by gluing it back together. We were never successful at hiding our damage, and one day my mother, in a fit of rage, exacted her revenge by plunging a chef's knife into the basketball, leaving it on the driveway like a piece of lifeless and flat roadkill.

Clare calls to me, "What's wrong?"

I throw off my shoes and pants and stomp upstairs. "Of all the days to step in dog shit it has to be today."

I hear Clare say from downstairs, "I've told you not to go out in the yard with your nice clothes. You always get something dirty."

I do not reply and continue my ranting, "The entire backyard and the damn dogs pick the end of the walkway to take a morning crap. If I did not know better, I would think the dogs are taking a passive-aggressive approach to retaliate against me for some past wrongdoing."

Clare rolls her eyes at me, and I resist the urge to admit she's right. I always assume the worst, that everyone—even the dog—is trying to teach me a lesson. It is another part of my past, a deep-seated mistrust ingrained into my psyche.

Eventually I get myself changed and I hurry to work. As I drive, my head buzzes and my heart races. I feel like an animal headed toward the slaughterhouse, Mr. Graves's office. It was my own fault for dillydallying out in the yard, but who could blame me?

Outside Mr. Graves's office I feel my hands shake as perspiration builds in my palms. I pull at my collar as I take a few deep breaths to ease my tension. Mr. Graves has a knack for bullying while seeming to act professional. A master at isolating his prey, Mr. Graves leaves no record of what is said or what occurs. I know this, because I exist on the other side of his behavior, helping others bludgeoned by his heavy hand despite their intent to do the right thing.

Mr. Graves's door opens. He walks out with a physician. Each wears a greedy smile as Mr. Graves slaps the doctor on the back and, in a giddy voice says, "Great seeing you again. I look forward to working with you. Appreciate your business."

On the physician's coat I see "Central Neurology Associates." No doubt, he is a doctor newly recruited by Mr. Graves to push the sale of RemMem. The physician's long white coat evokes my mother's unfulfilled dreams for me. She always wanted me to be a doctor. Like with tennis, I never lived up to her expectations or, as she would put it, I "never lived up to my talent." I try to focus on the task at hand, leaving the past where it should stay—in the past.

Mr. Graves passes me on the way back to his office without a flicker of acknowledgment. I overhear him on the phone with the chief strategy officer. "Yeah, I just struck a deal with Central Neurology. I could do this all day. You know, go around town cutting deals with doctors."

His assistant catches me listening and jumps up and closes the door. I massage the bridge of my nose with my thumb and index finger to clear the thousand thoughts pouring through my mind. One thought stubbornly stays with me: *Will I have a job after this?*

I wait. The annoying clicking of the assistant's typing fills the room. Each keystroke a thump on my aching head. I close my eyes when, without stopping, she says, "Mr. Graves will see you now." She does not get up.

My knees wobble when I walk to the door. My clammy palm leaves a smudge on the brass doorknob. As I walk in, I hear a gruff, "Hello, John."

Unlike other times when I walk into his office, Mr. Graves does not get up. Instead, he sits at his desk. Beside him is a small glass bottle of French sparkling water. He is looking down, signing papers with a Montblanc pen. He looks up at me and points to his meeting table. "You can take a seat over there."

I sit and, before I can open my notepad, Mr. Graves leans back in his leather desk chair, places his hands behind his head, and starts in. "Now, John, I don't think you understand how I control this board of directors and keep order. I don't need you pumping them full of misguided notions that we have done something wrong."

I begin to open my mouth, but before any words come out, Mr. Graves holds up his finger and continues, "John, you need to sit and just listen. I will not tolerate someone causing unnecessary friction among this board. You know as well as I do every pharmaceutical company is doing the exact same thing as we are doing. It's how we run our business, and the government needs to just stay out."

Just as I've always done with my mother, I nod my head and reply, "Yes, I understand."

"And regardless, I have a general counsel who supports what we are doing and is willing to fight anyone making these outlandish allegations. As a matter of fact, he is recommending that the company challenge this subpoena in court before replying. So, all that you need to do is share that the company received a subpoena. Don't speculate and for the love of God don't summarize what the government thinks."

"Yes, sir."

Mr. Graves stands up and walks over to me. As he looks down at me, his brief intentional silence unnerves me. My heart sinks. He says in a low, but sharp voice, "John, I know you are smart enough to know how much your family depends on your job. Now, when do you meet with the chairman?"

Browbeaten by his last statement, I submit and reply, "The day after tomorrow."

Mr. Graves can see from the look on my face he has won. "Good, I am glad you understand. Before the end of the day, I want you to rewrite your report and send it back to me."

I lower my head and say, "Yes, sir."

Before I can get out of my chair Mr. Graves yells out to his assistant, "Get me the chairman on the phone."

I gather my belongings and hurry out of the office. As I stand outside of the office sorting things in my work bag and in my head, I hear Mr. Graves call, "John! You still out there?"

"Yes, sir."

"The chairman says to meet him at the club the day after tomorrow."

I take a deep breath. I do not know if my sigh is relief or sarcasm.

Back in my office, I loathe my situation. *Mr. Graves is right. I cannot afford anything else.*

I give little thought to rewriting the memo. I add what Mr. Graves expects, short and to the point, and delete the rest. Before leaving for home, I email it to Mr. Graves. Before I get into my car he responds, "This is much better."

Vivian greets me when I arrive home. Her shimmering eyes are filled with water. "I am sorry, Daddy. I cut your flowers because I am making Mommy a bouquet for Mother's Day."

I swallow the lump in my throat. "That's OK. I think Mommy will love her flowers from you." I give Vivian a hug and we walk into the den together. After greeting everyone I sit oddly on the sofa and get to work on my iPhone.

"How was your day?" asks Clare.

I do not respond until I finish with my iPhone. "Sorry, I just realized I had not gotten my mother anything for Mother's Day and needed to order something tonight. Otherwise, it will not arrive until next week and once again I will have not lived up to her expectations of me."

CHAPTER SEVEN

The Pinnacle Country Club sits inconspicuously visible from the road. No sign announces its presence. Its members consist of a hierarchy of old families and blue bloods embodying conservative traditions of another time. The club, a century old, holds an impeccable reputation for privilege.

I enter its driveway lined by dogwood trees and stop at the valet desk. The Greek revival columns stand ominous and two large glossy ferns sit in large terracotta pots by the double doors like centurions. A young man dressed in a dark suit waits for me. He opens the door and parks my car. Inside, I walk to the hostess table. The young lady, Susie, looks down her nose at me. I say, "I am here to meet Mr. Arden."

"Right this way," she replies and walks over to Mr. Arden's table, swaying her hips with each step. Susie reminds me of a friend from high school named Suzanne.

Suzanne's family came from Shoals Mill, too. Unlike my family, her family took a different path to escape the past: behind-the-scenes deals, clandestine favors, and, when necessary, illicit relations. My family, too proud and too modest, seethed with jealousy as her family climbed the social ladder and mine did not.

Suzanne's grandmother and Hazel were friends and longtime coworkers from the Shoals Mill spinning room, having worked side by side for years. Suzanne and I attended the same church, too. She had a cheerful personality coupled with obvious confidence. Unlike the other high school girls who needed long, straight hair plunging over their shoulders, she showed off cobalt black hair that never even touched her neck. She was petite with a dainty nose and the shape of her lips gave a slight inviting pout. I imagined her lips tasted sweet like nectar from a lilac bloom.

Regardless of how her beauty captivated me as a teenager, my mother forbade me to date her, claiming, "She is too fast and not the type of girl for you." As a result, my romance with her was nothing more than a fantasy made real by a few conversations at school and giving Suzanne car rides to high school and church events. In exchange, I received nothing more than a hug from her, and from my mother, appreciation for my compliance with her wishes, just like the approval I received from Mr. Graves.

Before I sit, Susie leans over the table. Mr. Arden attempts to discreetly look down her low-cut dress. Seeing him do this, Susie smiles back at him and asks, "Mr. Arden, do you care for another drink?"

I wonder how many times they have rendezvoused for a tryst in the club's fabled fourth floor room for Mr. Arden to embrace his artificial youth, and Susie to hold tight to his false promises.

"Yes, Susie. And more blue cheese stuffed olives, too."

She takes his empty martini glass as Mr. Arden raises his hand to me and says, "Please, John, take a seat and have a drink."

I sit down and reply, "No thanks, Mr. Arden. I am going back to the office afterward."

He cocks his head and chuckles. "So am I."

We order lunch and after a little awkward small talk, Mr. Arden begins, "John, I understand we received a subpoena from the Department of Justice?"

"Yes, sir. They are inquiring about our speaker program for RemMem. I have contacted the lead investigator at the Department of Justice named in the subpoena. He was not shy about telling me how Cogniv-Pharma is the focus of their investigation."

Mr. Arden scratches his chin and replies, "I remember the board discussing the implementation of the program. It did not seem like a problem then. Why is it now?"

I glance around the room to avoid making eye contact and begin, "Well, sir," I stare above his head and continue, "I remember it being discussed at a board meeting. However, I am only invited to the meetings each quarter to give the compliance update. I do know there were several compliance-related memos circulated." Self-preservation makes me stop there and not remined him how the memos were sent to him and to Mr. Graves, as well as the entire board of directors.

Mr. Arden leans back in his chair and winks at Susie as she brings over our lunch. She places the plates in front of us and asks, "Will there be anything else?" Even though Susie is a hostess, Mr. Arden has instructed the club that only she will serve his table; and, of course, given who he is, they comply.

Mr. Arden grins and replies, "Maybe later."

Something catches Mr. Arden's attention, and I notice his caramel spray tan as he waves at a man in a dark suit who is entering the dining room. I recognize him as a federal judge for the district. He comes over and Mr. Arden says, "John, let me introduce you to a good friend of mine." I stand up as Mr. Arden says, "This is Judge Banks."

We exchange greetings and handshakes.

"How were things at the beach last week? Enjoy the resort?" asks Mr. Arden.

"Yes, I did. You run a spectacular resort. The wife and I had a great time."

"Good," replies Mr. Arden. "Glad to hear that. It's available anytime you like."

I sit at a loss for words. As the judge leaves for his table, Mr. Arden turns to me and says, "He's a great guy. I got him elected."

I wrinkle my face and say with false innocence, "I thought federal judges were appointed."

Mr. Arden winks, adjusts his diamond cuff links, and says, "You know what I mean."

We begin to eat, and I attempt to restart our conversation. "Now, Mr. Arden, about this subpoena. When the program was introduced, there were several regulatory risks identified to the board by management." Again, self-preserving, I do not acknowledge I wrote the memos.

Mr. Arden's voice becomes patronizing. "John, there are risks to everything and I am sure there are risks associated with this, too. However, I am not worried, and I will give you two reasons why. First, I have already discussed this with our general counsel, and he says that, like every ethics officer, you are overreacting. Second, every damn pharmaceutical company in America is doing the same thing we are doing."

I remain silent and look out the large dining room window overlooking the veranda. Beyond the veranda a group of teenage boys play tennis. My glance turns to a stare until Mr. Arden interrupts, "You play tennis?"

"I played a lot when I was younger. I played in college, too."

"Do you still play, or did you quit?"

"I stopped playing."

I do not expect Mr. Arden to detect my subtle evasion of the subject or appreciate the difference. I do not enjoy talking about my days playing tennis. Instead, I prefer to bury it deep within myself.

The remainder of the lunch is silent. I need nothing more to understand his expectations, so I spend my time staring at the tennis courts and recalling the pain and struggles.

The most important tournament each year, the Palmetto Championships, always takes place during the first week right after the last day of the school year. It is the qualifying tournament for the southern regionals. A higher regional ranking would mean a greater likelihood of a scholarship, but first I would have to win enough matches in the Palmetto Championships to qualify.

Weeks before the tournament I train and practice each day while friends talk about their upcoming plans for First Week at Myrtle Beach. I devote mornings to conditioning by running up to three miles and dedicate afternoons to playing practice matches on the courts at the Cardinal Racquet Club. As every year, each adult I play compliments me, "You are playing the best I have ever seen," "You are at another level," and, "I expect you will go far in this year's Palmetto Championships." Worse, expectations, and especially my mother's expectations, grow even more when, a few days before the tournament, the local newspaper calls to interview me.

The Palmetto Championships always finds its home in Belton, South Carolina, where tennis etched its mark deep into the town's mystical fabric. The town has hosted the tournament for the last half century. What makes the tournament unlike any other is how matches are played on private courts at family homes throughout town and the municipal courts in the middle of town.

Belton was only ten miles from home. This always made me anxious because people I knew would come over to watch the matches. Worse, this year, there was a part of me that wanted to be at Myrtle Beach with my friends.

The day before the tournament starts, we make the short drive to Belton to review the drawsheet of the sixty-four players and to see who I would be playing. When we arrive, as usual there are several mothers of players there who speak to us. "Hi, Francis. How have the Greenburns been?"

My mother is always polite but holds herself in a defensive posture. Crossing her arms, she replies, "We are doing pretty well. Glad school is over."

"Yes, us, too. Did I see y'all won another state championship?"

My mother's face brightens for a moment, "We did. Five to four over Myrtle Beach High School. John and his doubles partner won the deciding match, breaking the four-to-four tie."

This small talk continues as others ask if I had played any tournaments this year. "Yes," my mother replies with a blunt voice. "Things did not go well in Aiken."

I look over my mother's shoulders and look at the drawsheet. I find myself seeded fifth, the highest seed I have achieved at the Palmetto Championships. It suggests I am currently the fifth best player in the state. I attribute this to my strong showing last winter at the southern indoor, though it might have been higher were it not for the setback in Aiken. I notice I am matched against a player in the first round to whom I have never lost.

Back in the car my mother relaxes. I see the tense muscles in my mother's face ease. No longer grimacing, she says, "Did you see the diamond ring Brian's mother was wearing? I bet it is at least three karats. I hear her husband gave her the choice of having a new BMW or a diamond ring."

I match my mother's liveliness and reply, "I would have taken the car."

"Oh, son," my mother replies as she rolls her eyes, "You should always take the diamond. Diamonds last forever."

She continues, "Anyway, your father says her husband was a drunk in college. He was on the basketball team and your father says teammates had to search the bars to find him before basketball games. I bet he still drinks and bought that diamond out of guilt."

On the day of my first match of the tournament, I sit in my bedroom and listen to classical music. Vivaldi's "Spring" fills the air—an attempt to unwind my nerves. From the chest of drawers, the top covered with trophies from tournaments in the ten, twelve, and fourteen divisions, I pull out my favorite pair of Nike shorts and match it with my high school state championship T-shirt. I open my closet and grab my three Prince Classic Graphite rackets. I carefully examine each to test the wear and tension of the strings. Next, I inspect the grips. Satisfied, I put them into my tennis travel bags along with a few extra T-shirts and a hand towel. I grab my water cooler and head to the car where my mother awaits.

As my mother drives us to the tournament, I sit in the front seat and watch the railroad tracks running parallel to the road. Like Shoals, Belton is another mill town. The railroad tracks predate the roads and lead through town and to the old mills that, like the town of Shoals, bear witness to a bygone era and to the place where my world and my mother's collide.

My mother fills the silence of our ride: "You know you have beaten this guy five or six times and never lost to him."

Her talking makes me nervous, and I wish to remain quiet. However, I appease her and say, "Yes, Mom." My mind begins to wonder about the great time my friends must be having at the beach.

My mother continues, "You have more talent than this guy and anyone else in the tournament."

I cringe at the words coming from my mother's mouth. I do not understand why she thinks I possess such talent. Worse, I know that most of our family's money goes toward playing tennis and losing feels like squandering it all. Butterflies began to fill my stomach. I try to recall the music I listened to at home. I need to relax. A useless tactic because my mother continues talking about me all the way to Belton. Nothing seems to block her constant droning.

We arrive and my match is on the main courts in Belton. I feel like the entire tournament is watching me. I am confident, but my hands are shaky during the warm-up. The match begins and I am playing well, but the score is close, and I have never had a close match with this opponent. I lose the first set and panic sets in. I look over at my mother. She wears her familiar look of frustration with me that she always has when I am losing. During the break, as we change sides of the court, I sit and close my eyes. I collect myself, but still think, *How is this happening? I have never lost to this guy.*

The second set begins, and I get off to a fast start, winning the first three games. My mother looks more relaxed, which lessens the pressure I feel. I win the second set and welcome the ten-minute break before beginning the third set.

During the break I see my high school tennis coach working behind the tournament desk. It is an undeniable fact she and my mother do not get along. Clear and simple, my mother disapproves of my coach allowing me to make my own mistakes, like at the high school tournament at Hilton Head. My mother allowed me for the first time on such a trip to stay with the team, while she stayed in a different hotel. During the night, my friends on the team and I stayed out late, roaming the beach and condo pool looking for girls. The next day I lost both my matches. As a result, my mother made me stay in the hotel with her, leaving my teammates and the fun behind at the condo. It was just how things were with my mother, straightforward and unavoidable.

I am not sure, but I think the next Monday my mother called the high school principal to complain about her perception that there was a lack of supervision. My mother was always direct and firm, making sure her point was clear.

After I refill my water cooler, I walk over to her and say, "Hi, Coach Sandy. I didn't know you were working the tournament."

"Yes," she replies." How are you doing?"

"I am in the middle of a match and getting ready to start my third set," I answer as I take a long drink of water.

She interrupts me: "Third set! You better get your butt back out there."

I go back to the court, without stopping to speak to my mother, and begin the third set. I am hitting the ball hard and playing aggressively. However, the harder I hit the ball the stronger it comes back across the court against me. My opponent has never played this well against me. I begin to think, *I have never lost in the first round of this tournament, and I have always qualified for the regionals.*

We continue battling. The sun sits high in the late morning sky as the humidity rises with the pressure I am feeling. My clothes are drenched and my feet on the hard baked court feel like I am walking on hot coals. Halfway through the third set we are tied at four games apiece. I attempt to remain confident, yet I think losing in the first round will make it very hard to qualify for the southern regionals. My mother has moved off the bleachers and perches herself near the court with her arms crossed. She leans forward, like a starved raptor ready to swoop down on its weak prey.

The pressure she adds to the match is too much for me. Anger and frustration set in. I cannot manage my emotions. I start hitting the ball harder. My body begins to behave strangely. I am nervous about losing and my heart beats in uneven patterns, shooting up and down like a flying acrobat in the circus. My brain becomes stagnant, like when the neighborhood ponds become covered with algae. I cannot think. I lose the next two games and the match. The other players watching the match cheer at my opponent's victory as I shake hands. I feel lonely and give a longing gaze to the sky.

I have never lost in the first round. My heart, once brimming earlier, full of excitement, feels empty. Disappointment settles heavy upon my shoulders, pressing me down as I walk in defeat toward the car, where my mother waits in angry silence.

In the car I see how my mother's rigid posture announces her disappointment. She releases her clenched jaw enough to sigh and say, "If you had come over to see me during the break, I could have told you how to win the third set. Instead, you decided to act cute and go over to Coach Sandy. You are wasting my time and money trying to be cute. You have potential to be a great player, but you are throwing away your opportunity. God has given you all this talent and it is a sin for you to waste it."

The word "cute" cuts into my skin like a dull, rusty knife. The ride home stays silent, but the tension hangs heavy in the air. I think about the missed opportunity for a scholarship offer. Worse, other players at the tournament were already receiving letters from college coaches. A stark reminder of my shortcomings.

The Palmetto Championships is double elimination and for the remainder of the tournament, I consciously stay close to my mother. It is her desire, and I do not want to upset her. I avoid interacting with other players or my high school coach. I feel weak and embarrassed. But I do what my mother wants, and it is easier to comply than risk the guilt that comes with nonconformity.

In the consolation round of the Palmetto Championships, I win three consecutive matches. Now, facing a lower ranked opponent, I know my mother will only accept winning. A few middle-aged men I often practice with come over to Belton to watch my match. As the match begins to unfold, I begin to struggle, gripped by the anxiety swelling throughout my body.

The cloudless sky sends its relentless heat. The small pine trees beside the court stand motionless, and the birds do not sing. The stifling humidity sucks my energy. I feel the sun baking through layers of my skin. My mind turns into mush, and dehydration begins to set in. My nerves take control of my mind and body and threaten to overwhelm me.

The third set tiebreaker ends with exhaustion and my double fault.

My opponent's father hollers, "Now, maybe my son will get the respect he deserves." I do not understand his excitement.

At the same time, one of the middle-aged men says to my mother, "Your son has so much talent, but he does not know what to do with it."

I overhear his words, and they make me cry. I sit on the court with a towel over my head, hiding my emotions. *If I do not know what to do with it, why does someone not tell me how?*

I gather my gear and walk to the car. Disappointed, I remind myself I have won enough matches to qualify for the southern regionals.

My mother gets in the car and slams the door.

Her frustration exasperates me. I demand, "Why are you mad? I'm the one who lost."

She jerks the gearshift into reverse and swerves around with such force it throws me into the passenger-side door. She flips the gearshift to drive and frowns at me. "God has given you so much talent. No one did anything for me, but everything, your talent, has been given to you. I have sacrificed so much. You will never understand!"

I lower my head. My mother stomps on the accelerator. "You never play up to your talent!"

I do not understand what that means.

She continues, "Why do you waste your talent? Do you enjoy being average? Let me show you average."

We speed across town to the mill hill where she and my father grew up. As she drives, my mother points to the small homes with rickety steps and front porches falling in, like loaves of bread that have been taken out of the oven too soon. Paint is peeling from the sides of the houses, and porches are missing boards. Rusted cars sit in dirt driveways. Stray dogs roam. Grass grows around abandoned home appliances—dishwashers, refrigerators, and ovens. Their presence, further testament to the financial failure of the families living on the mill hill.

My mother, with hawklike attention, points out where family members live. Most are distant relatives, but it does not matter. "Is this where you want to spend your life? I have sacrificed everything for you to do better than this!"

My mother lived vicariously through me in a privacy of pain. Somehow, I was supposed to mend her pain.

Never once did my mother acknowledge how, regardless of my loss on the tennis court, I still qualified for the southern regional invitational tournament in Atlanta, Georgia. Although I secured a place in the bottom five grouping, it signified I ranked as one of the top sixteen players in South Carolina.

For me this was good enough, but it was *not good enough* for my mother.

CHAPTER EIGHT

After lunch, I return to my office unsure of myself. My heart and mind continue their battle between thinking and feeling. One moral. One safe. Both justified.

My father calls me, again. Although I have an older brother, my father's calls to him about my mother stopped long ago. Like my mother, he is blunt and straightforward, always telling my father, "Just put her in a home if she's too difficult to handle." I have forever been seen as the sensitive son. My mother used to see it as a flaw, thinking it held me back on the tennis court, always demanding, "John, you need to be more aggressive like your brother." Now, my father sees it as a blessing, a voice of reason in his darkest hours with my mother.

As usual my father does not say hello. "John, this is your dad. This medicine for your mom. The one for her memory." He pauses and I hear him yell, "What?" My mother is shouting at him in the background as my father attempts to continue. "Hold on, John. Wait. Wait a minute."

He puts the phone down and I hear him say, "Francis, I am trying to talk to John, and I can't hear over your hollering."

I hear my mom yelling, "Damn it! How the hell are you going to hear him if you put the phone down?"

I hear my father walking to the next room. He picks up the phone again and stutters, "I-I-I… This memory pill… It's not working."

I silently release my disappointment.

My father places the phone on a table. I cannot hear much other than my mother yelling, "Why don't you just go back to the mill hill?"

For a moment I think, *What is it about Shoal Mills and why does it continue to haunt her?*

My father picks up the phone and I attempt persistence. "Dad, it's only been three days. Give it time. It should eventually work."

He replies, "This, this, isn't going to work."

In the background, I hear my mother continuing her rant, "Will you just shut the hell up. I don't have a memory problem, and you can kiss my ass if you think so."

Early afternoon and my mother was already tempestuous. I relent. "Dad just don't worry about it. You can't force her to take it."

There are just some things you cannot change.

I sense my father's immediate relief from his burden. Before he ends the call, I hear my mother yell one last time, "I'm not crazy!"

My father, in a way only he could, always understood my mother and appreciated her, making life, at times, simpler for me. He always provided moments of innocence, allowing an escape from tennis, like the time drove me home from a tennis lesson and, as we crossed the bridge into the neighborhood, he exclaimed, "Holy cow! Look at that snapping turtle crossing the road."

I looked out the window and saw the large reptile crawling across the street between the two ponds.

My father pulled the car over between the ponds and parked. We got out and observed its prehistoric-looking bony plated shell. We circled to its front. It stopped and looked at us with a mean look of disgust, showing it was ready to snap its hooked upper jaw at us and take out a piece of flesh. My father baited the turtle's posturing and attitude by lowering my tennis racket toward its face. Without warning and in a flash of a moment, the turtle snapped its jaws and sent a crack across the frame of the racket. My father raised the racket, and we stood in amazement as we slowly walked away in awe of the turtle's power. The turtle, content with his work, continued his creep across the road from one pond to the next and we returned to the car.

In this moment, the world was reduced to the marvel of a creature's slow journey and tennis was a distant memory, until back in the car I was reminded of my mother's overbearing nature when my father said, "John, don't tell your mother about this. I will buy you a new racket this afternoon."

I nodded in agreement as my wide eyes examined the broken racket.

Long-suffering from my mother's outbursts, my father could not have been a better husband. He possessed limitless patience and dedication to those he loved, especially my mother. They have been together since the eighth grade, sixty-six years. The last five, intense. Time, never a savior, especially when the past becomes the present.

The next day in the early morning before work, I sit in my home office surrounded by things that comfort me: my collection of books, a watercolor of daisies painted by my grandmother, and Delta blues lyrics streaming from my computer.

Hazel, our black Lab, sits as a guardian at my feet. I remember how I protested when the kids first decided on her name. "My grandmother's name was Hazel," I exclaimed, "You can't name a dog after my grandmother. That's sacrilegious!" The children merely laughed at this remark and handed me the small, wriggling puppy, who immediately licked my face, a baptism of innocence and acceptance.

I lean down to Hazel, now an adult dog. She rises and uses her forepaw to hold my head still while licking my face with the same lavish affection she did as a puppy. Her gritty forepaw stirs memories of my grandmother Hazel's arthritic hands grabbing my face for a kiss and how her thick nails and gem-encrusted rings scratched my cheeks. Both Hazels are synonymous with unconditional love and their touch is a reminder of connections that transcend time.

Clare opens the office door. I see her worried look. She steps into the room and with a voice full of apprehension says, "I just spoke with your father. We had a long conversation about your mother. It's wearing him down. I am really worried about him."

Clare, a nurse, often finds herself at the receiving end of my father's telephone calls, especially when he deems my responses insufficient. In my eyes, Clare possesses a rare gift, making impossible things appear effortless and natural. When her gaze, gentle and understanding, falls on my father, or her soft voice reaches his ears, it gives him the warmth of a daughter he never had. Quite a contrast from having sons, as if having sons meant unemotional indifference.

I knew calling this early meant my father was more worried than usual. Subdued, I reply, "It's wearing me down, too, and I am not even there. I have been having difficulty focusing this morning, between last night's call and everything at work."

Clare looks at the blank computer screen and then back at me. "I am sure this is emotionally draining for you." She leans in and places her hand on my shoulder. "However, we need to go see them at the end of this week. Your dad needs a break."

A train whistle blows in the distance. I bite my lip. My reluctance keeps me from answering. The computer flashes the receipt of an email. I read it out of avoidance. When I finish, I lean back in my chair and place both hands behind my head.

"Well, we might as well go. Mr. Graves and Mr. Arden have postponed the compliance report until next month's board meeting." I release my hands and look at the ceiling. "What bullshit," I exclaim as I release a chuckle, like an idiot, but pain-filled. "As long as this matter remains in the air, they would be crazy to fire me."

For the remainder of the week, awkwardness covers everything at work, like a low-lying fog. I wonder if I am the only one who can see the truth. Lonesome, I feel a shadow of isolation over my head. My coworkers know nothing and remain oblivious. The general counsel deepens this void by not replying to my emails and leaving phone messages unanswered.

Mr. Graves and Mr. Arden, I am certain, are undoubtedly executing a Machiavellian plan to exonerate themselves, leaving others to suffer the burdens of their misdeeds. Their fortune and fame have been forged on the profits of Cogniv-Pharma. They know prison hangs in the balance but have escaped the labyrinth of the judicial system many times. Together, they dwell in a tangled web of compromised moral principles, their power built on the ruins of others.

I read the subpoena again. Nothing new stands out, but I begin to wonder if, like with my mother, there are deeper truths concealed beneath the thin surface.

C H A P T E R   N I N E

Interstate 85—we drive across the Vandiver Bridge above the Savannah River and exit the interstate just a few miles inside the South Carolina border by Lake Hartwell. I breathe in the cool Upstate air as we pass the distinctive red hills of the South Carolina Piedmont. Seeing the red hills reminds me of my boyhood, a time before tennis, when I spent days digging and collecting mica before coming home with socks and shoes caked in the red mud. "This will never wash out," I remember my mother saying. The following week, the rust-colored socks sit in the trash can.

After a few minutes we cross another body of water, one of the ponds of my old neighborhood. The spring drought exposes each ponds' muddy red banks, but the water is flat and smooth, making reflections beam like a mirror.

As the car crosses the small bridge over the larger of the two ponds in my old neighborhood, I see a belted kingfisher sitting deliberately conspicuous on a branch hanging over the neighborhood pond. It flashes its steely blue-gray shaggy crest. It surveys the water below, preparing to dive with its spear-shaped bill and evoke Cherokee healing ceremonies. Along the bank, Canada geese rest in the grass. Soon, they will take to the skies and fly north to their summer home.

All of this is formative geography, a landscape etched in the depths of my being. I long to be here, despite the discomfort memory brings. It is hard not to be captivated by the land and what it holds not just for me, but for my family.

My childhood home sits in a middle-class neighborhood of ordinary two-story ranch and split-level houses. Banal front yards provide venues for neighborhood football and baseball games, driveways have basketball goals, and backyards swing sets. Station wagons and family SUVs adorn the driveways.

Before we arrive, I know my mother has ensured her house looks immaculate. Every day, she and my father vacuum the carpet, mop the tile, and dust the wood. My father polishes the dining room chairs we never use. He waxes the wood floors in the living room, where no one sits or visits. My mother uses a comb to straighten the carpet fringe.

Years ago, my mother sought to vanquish her mill heritage, transforming our home into a facsimile of pictures from *Southern Living*. She hired the same interior designer renowned for his work decorating homes for the Parade of Homes. When he finished there were no grand brick porticos, no oversized front doors, no sprawling green lawns, and no formal gardens filled with herbs for gourmet cooking. Instead, our house became adorned with Chinese jars and foreign patterns casting an illusion of a refined and cultured way of life. Wood floors and "Persian" rugs, purchased at discount outlets, replaced the shag carpet. My mother meticulously mounted crown molding throughout the house. Each picture is hung exactly twenty-four inches below it. The herb garden resides in a cracked clay pot spilling over on the patio.

During the renovations, the decorator looked at the unadorned wooden mantle over the fireplace said, "Your fireplace mantle looks like something installed by Daniel Boone." Afterward, he replaced it with scalloped Venetian plaster sconces complemented by a faux antique bronze finish and adorned by a verdigris mantle.

Next, he suggested painting the house a washed-out shade of pink. The paint provides an unexpected vibrant kick that is too much. Our house takes on a pink hue. When asked, my mother corrects everyone. "It's Bermuda coral," she insists.

I pull the car into the driveway, and my mother's appearance jumps out at me. Instead of her usual name brand ensemble, she wears her housecoat and slippers. I recognize her angry, stiff gait, both fists on her hips, from past days at tennis tournaments. She turns to see us. Her brow, still furrowed, shows she remains in fight mode.

"What's Grammy mad about?" asks Mary.

"Beats me." I look to the next yard and see the next-door neighbor, Bobby, using his blower to clear leaves and debris from his driveway.

Before I respond, Katie asks, "Why is Grammy already in her housecoat and slippers? It's only four."

My mother gives a brief look of confusion toward the car until she realizes it is us. She smiles and embraces each child one by one as they get out of the car. I open the back and begin unpacking, wondering if my mother's current appearance means her health decline has worsened. My suspicion is confirmed when I come around to greet my mother and she bursts out, "It is a good thing you got here when you did. I was about to kick Bobby's ass."

Before she can hug me, I ask, "What on earth for?"

"Watch 'im. He is always blowing his trash and shit into my flower beds. I just can't stand him."

I hug my mother and say, "Mom, let's go inside. I can unload the car later," as I use one arm to guide her into the house and away from Bobby.

As we walk to the front porch, I glance back at Bobby and give a careful wave. He smiles and waves back. I follow my mother up the front porch steps, but before we go inside, I say, "Mom, you go on inside. I forgot something in the car."

She goes inside. Bobby sees me walking back to the car and turns off his blower. We meet at the back of the car to remain hidden from my mother.

Bobby smiles and says, "I heard you all were coming into town."

"Yeah," I respond. "Sounds like my dad needs a break, so we decided to come up for a long weekend."

Bobby scratches his head. "Yeah, things have been kinda bad. It's like the last few weeks she has gotten a lot worse."

"What do you mean?"

"Well, the other day, your mom and dad were outside, and she started in on him about cutting the grass. She started yelling and cussing at him, and the next thing I know, I see your mom out in the backyard pushing the mower. She was not looking where she was going and ran over a sprinkler connected to the irrigation system. Water started spewing up in the air, and your dad came out cussing up a storm. I helped him shut off the water, but your mom gave him hell."

Bobby is the neighbor my parents love to fuss about, but the first person they call when they need help.

"Oh Jesus!" I reply. "That must have been a sight." I shake my head and say, "Well, I better get inside before they come looking for me. Thanks for helping them."

Bobby smiles and says, "It's no problem. I know it's hard getting old."

I go inside. My father looks at me and says, "Hey! Where have you been?"

"I forgot something in the car."

"Bobby still out there?"

I give my father a puzzled look. "Yes. What's this about Mom and Bobby?"

"Your mom is pissed."

"About what?"

"Bobby."

"Yes, Dad. I know that. What did he do?"

"He blows his yard debris into our yard."

Exasperated, I exclaim, "You don't really believe that. Do you?"

"Well, your mother has seen him. Anyway, if he does not stop going through our mail, I am going to kick his ass before your mother does."

"What?"

"Yeah, he's taking my mail."

"What do you mean, taking your mail?"

"The other day, he was standing at our mailbox with his hand in it."

I roll my eyes and sigh. "That does not mean he was taking something. Maybe he got some of your mail, and he was putting it back. Maybe he was missing something and thought the postman put it in your box."

"John, Bobby is full of shit, and I don't trust him."

I put down the suitcases and turn to go back to the car. As I walk out of the house, I look in the living room. Everything is in the same place as it was forty years ago, even the upright piano no one has played since I left home.

When we arrive home from the Palmetto Champions, I open the mailbox in hopes of seeing a letter from a college coach. Empty. My mother goes inside and up to her bedroom. I hear her crying throughout the day. I do not understand what she mourns.

By the evening, she sits on the couch, still sulking at the day's loss. Her presence makes me uneasy, and I go into the living room and play the piano.

My father arrives home from work. I continue to play as he attempts to console my mother.

She laments, "We have such an ordinary life. We are just common mill hill ordinary."

My mother begins yelling at my father. I play louder to drown out the battle of emotions that ensues.

Guilt is always her offensive strategy. I hear her yell, "Look at all I have sacrificed for this family to make our lives better?" My father does not reply, or at least I do not hear him. Whatever he does or says is unsatisfactory. This causes my mother to feel that her initial onslaught of guilt was unsuccessful. As a result, she reinforces her arsenal and, unlike her guided, precise shots of guilt, her secondary attack attempts to overwhelm him with a saturation of emotions. It is like watching a 1980s daytime soap.

She continues, "My heart hurts! Someone may need to take me to the hospital." Now in sight of the living room I see her reeling about, clutching her hair, and breathing with long intentional huffs and puffs. She grabs her stomach like she is going to vomit and begins retching. It is like watching a daytime soap. She turns and goes upstairs. The bedroom door slams. My father, the peacekeeper, sits in the next room. He does not follow her upstairs. He remains quiet. He knows the shame of the past is too deep to soothe.

The battle is over, and I play one last piece.

From an early age I would always play the piano when my parents argued. I do not remember their arguments, other than their intense length, except my mother always accused my dad of not being able to communicate with her. Typically, she included a demand that he either "get with the program or just go back to the mill hill."

Once, I remember my parents arguing past midnight. After the argument was over, they went and ate midnight breakfast at Waffle House. When they returned home, I remember them laughing, "John, you should have seen all the drunks at Waffle House trying to sober up."

Music soothed me during my parents' arguments by taking me to a place far away from their conflict. My mom did not understand this. She just laughed and told people like my piano teacher, "Piano is just an emotional outlet for John, especially when his father and I argue."

CHAPTER TEN

After dinner, the night grows dark. We all convene in the family room. As we talk, my mother gets tired and begins repeating herself. She forgets names and places. She has trouble finishing sentences.

My father says to her, "Francis, can you not see that you are repeating yourself?" I know my father's fatigue makes him weary and causes him to give in to his frustration.

I close my eyes and sigh. I have told my father a million times: Don't confront mom about this. Leave it alone. When she reaches this state, she gets defensive if you ask about or question her memory. Worse, she thinks you are calling her crazy, like her family, and it ignites her.

My mother responds by raising her head and yelling, "Shut the hell up and get me another glass of wine. I am not crazy."

The grief and chronic anxiety overtake reality and pull her into the past. Since the mill, her family has coped by drinking. A bottle later, mom slumps in her chair. I have seen my mother like this many times. My son has not. He asks me, "Has Grammy had too much to drink?"

"Yes, she has."

"Why?"

"She just has, Henry. It makes things easier for her."

"Grammy and Mom say that's why you play the piano at home."

"Yes, Henry, it makes things easier for me."

The next day at my parents' house I lay awake in bed and study the gray-painted walls in my bedroom. They have always been painted gray and I have always thought how gray, devoid of vibrancy, exudes a sense of hopelessness and discontent.

I get out of bed and walk downstairs. My mother and father sit at the breakfast room table. I pour a cup of coffee and join them. Mom gazes out into the backyard, holding a Pop-Tart. I say, "The breakfast of champions."

My father does not detect my sarcasm and asks, "You want something other than coffee? How about a Pop-Tart? We have strawberry or chocolate."

"No thanks, Dad," I reply. "I am fine with just coffee." I look and see him holding a chocolate chip cookie in his hand.

My parents never ate cereal and hated oatmeal and cream of wheat. I remember weekends when I was a child, my mother cooked bacon, sausage, and eggs, then complained about the mess. Now, they prefer something easy and sweet for breakfast that does not make a mess and keeps the stovetop pristine. I enjoy the opportunity for sarcasm their breakfast choices provide me with, but I think to myself, *They've made it this long together, so I guess they've earned the right to eat whatever they like, even if that means always filling the kids' bellies with sweet tea from sunrise to sunset.*

My mother admires the yard and says, "You know, I could just sit here all day. Seeing the ponds and enjoying the sunshine makes me feel like I am on a riverboat cruise. You know, you and Clare need to go on one of those riverboat cruises."

When I was two, my father's job took my entire family to France for six months so he could receive training. We spent weekends traveling across western Europe and enjoying ourselves in the small, quaint village we lived in. When we returned home, my parents brought with them six bottles of wine and two Swiss wall clocks as mementos. They never uncorked the wine, and my father unwittingly ruined the clocks by cleaning them with a silicone lubricant.

My mother often talks about Europe. She reminisces about her time there. Some days, like this one, she says, "I wish I could leave and live there for the rest of my life."

I do not respond and continue to sip my coffee. I am thankful my mother refrains from filling the silence with memories of tennis.

My mother starts to eat her second Pop-Tart. "You know, I could just sit here all day. Seeing the pond and enjoying the sunshine makes me feel like I am on a riverboat cruise. You know, you and Clare need to go on one of those riverboat cruises."

"Yes, you and Dad always enjoyed those cruises." My comment is sincere. They have traveled to every major river in Europe except the Danube. Dad recently purchased tickets and airfare for a Danube cruise. He canceled it. "Your mom is just too much to handle."

I grieve. My parents' travels in Europe have been some of their happiest times together, even if my mother escapes reality through dreams of living there.

My mom says again, "You know I could just sit here all day. Seeing the pond and enjoying the sunshine makes me feel like I am on a riverboat cruise. You know, you and Clare need to go on one of those riverboat cruises."

This is my mother's new reality; except she refuses to accept it.

My mother finishes her breakfast and heads to the refrigerator. She fills a cup with ice and water and begins stirring in her cappuccino mix. "I'm going to take this upstairs and get dressed." I listen to the rubber soles of her slippers slide against the tile as she shuffles her feet.

Once she is upstairs, my father leans in and says in his usual staccato voice, "John, your mother. It's gotten bad."

"No kidding, Dad. I have never seen her repeat herself this often. How long has this been going on?"

"It's just bad. I'm going to talk to someone. We need to move down to Florida, closer to where you live, and into a place where someone can help me with your mom. I have already picked out a place."

I moved away from my parents over thirty years ago. We have never lived nearby since. A somber reality circles my mind. I sip my coffee and examine my father's pensive expression. His downcast posture gives me doubt. "OK, tell me what you are thinking."

"John, listen, the last time we were in Florida, I went down to that residential living place and looked at an apartment. It's a nice one-bedroom apartment with a view of a lake. I think your mom will like it. You know how she loves watching the ocean when we go to the beach."

"Have you talked to Mom?" My father mentioned this possibility to her last year. She replied, "You can go anytime you like, so long as you don't mind being alone. I'm staying here."

My father clears his throat. "Not yet. I want you to help me with that."

Reluctantly, I say, "Yes, I can." I feel sympathy for my father and recognize his good intentions. At the same time, I feel caught in the horns of a dilemma. Like at work, I must unite opposites. I retreat inward.

A tear forms in my father's eye, giving him a glassy stare. "Give me a little time to think about this." The synapses of my brain sit still as the enormity of this task weighs on my heart like a millstone. I welcome anything to break the silence as my nerves continue to grind at hearing how my father plans to move my mother and himself to Florida, when suddenly, my mother shuffles into the kitchen. Her hair, still wet from a shower, hangs in wild waves. She wears no makeup. Her uncharacteristic look serves as a reminder of my daunting task. She opens the refrigerator and pulls out a wine bottle. When she reaches for a glass, I see the bulge of her stomach, ascites from the past years of drinking. I pull inward and say, "I think I will go for a walk."

As I leave the front door, I hear my father. "Francis, don't you think it is a little early?"

"I am just getting a little bit. My back is bothering me."

I retreat out the backyard to the neighborhood pond. A return to my refuge of the genuine. I have always sought peace and understanding at the pond. I see the vestiges of God, chattering ducks, frogs sitting on lily pads, and rows of turtles sunbathing on logs. A sanctuary of nature, a church in the wild, I listen to the ducks. I see a snake slithering its wide body on top of the water. Bees buzz around the blooming lily pads. The herons stand still like stone statues. I hear a frog take a leap of faith into the dark water, leaving the slightest expanding ripples on the water.

The pond is a theophany where my mind feels at home. A home of innocent human happiness and deep understanding I constantly yearn for.

I return from the pond, and the three girls are about to pile into the car. My mother sits in the front passenger seat with a Styrofoam cup of Diet Coke. I smile at them and ask, "Where are y'all off to?"

They reply in unison, "Poppy and Grammy are taking us to the goat farm. Grammy says they have baby goats, and we should buy one."

I give an obvious smirk and say, "Sure, bring back a goat. It can stay here with Grammy. And I am sure it will enjoy munching on her hydrangeas."

My mom hears the conversation, leans over as Mary opens the car door, and yells with slightly slurred words, "How many goats do you want us to bring back for you?"

I yell playfully, "No goats!" and then whisper to all three girls, "Please watch her. She is not very steady on her feet."

Henry, the oldest, is named after my father's father, who worked as an athletic director at Shoals Mill before retiring. Henry has always been sentimental and enjoys learning about his family. Henry and I take my father's car and drive across the railroad tracks to where Shoals Mill once stood.

Mill life, pure and simple, is now gone and forgotten. A giant padlock secures the mill doors. Kudzu vines creep over the mill's heaps of broken bricks lying naked in the sun. Shoals Mill is intentionally forgotten by many of its people. It broke hearts. Only a few hold on to cherished memories, and those who stayed, like my father's parents, say, "It was good to us."

Mill village memories converge on my soul. I see the mechanic's garage where Hazel ran over his battery charger. Rather than act disgusted, he consecrated its death with a beer. We go by the Snack Shop where my grandfather Henry showed me how to pour salted peanuts into a bottle of Mountain Dew. I recall the pinball machine and begging for change from the adults. Now, boards cover the windows.

I turn down Park Avenue. My father's parents' house is gone. It's now a vacant grassy knoll, sitting empty. I get out of the car and walk into the yard. I stand where the den formerly sat. The world seems silent, but if I listen closely, I can hear National Wrestling Alliance on TV and my uncle howling in delight. I can even smell the kitchen.

My father's parents' four-room mill house hosted many family gatherings. I remember the feeling of claustrophobia as a young boy searching for a place among the thirteen people convening for Sunday lunch. As an adult, I do not comprehend how my grandmother cooked dishes of macaroni and cheese, plates of biscuits, and bowls of black-eyed peas with one cooking range in a tiny kitchen and a small refrigerator with only an icebox.

Behind their house, the original mill church, Southern Baptist, still stands. Like everything, its windows are boarded, and the front door is fastened with a padlock. I remember the inside, the straight-back wooden pews holding the King James Bible and Broadman hymnals. The choir, blue-haired ladies, clothed in long head-to-toe white robes with golden stoles. The preacher dressed in a shiny three-piece suit bellowing out sermons filled with warnings about hell being hotter…skipping church…not reading your Bible and rejecting the Holy Spirit.

I drive down to Q Street, where my father's uncle Claude lived. The charred remains of his house sit as a reminder of the fire that consumed the roof and one side of the house. Great Uncle Claude was a mystery growing up. Our family talked about his service in World War II: a private in the Italian campaign under the command of General Patton. He does not say much about the war. I know nothing else about Claude except family whispers and rumors about his moonshining and cockfighting days when he was younger.

Everyone on the mill hill had a nickname. My paternal grandfather, Henry, was nicknamed Grinny. He wore an authentic grin. He made others feel good. He coached mill baseball and basketball teams. He dedicated his life to city recreation leagues and the Salvation Army Boys Club. If you grew up on the mill hill, at some time, Grinny coached you. He ensured each player got a uniform, a chance to bat, and a ride to and from the game.

Grinny and my grandmother were poor, but, as a child, I did not know. In the early 1980s, the government sent them two five-pound blocks of socialized cheese. Pale orange and pungent with an aftertaste of humiliation.

A few years after my grandfather's death, the Salvation Army Boys Club dedicated a baseball field at Shoals Mill in Grinny's name. Twenty-five years later, the ball field, like the mill, was abandoned and forgotten. The marker had fallen over and was covered with weeds and briars. Like the mill, it was forgotten until a former player named Fireball discovered it.

Grinny coached Fireball on the mill's twelve-and-under baseball team fifty-five years ago. He gave him the nickname, too. The newspaper ran an article about Fireball discovering the abandoned marker. "Back then, everyone who worked in the mill was family. We were a community, and we looked out for each other."

The article described how Fireball cleaned the marker, set it upright, and reinforced it so that it would remain in place. "Coach deserves that. He was a daddy to all of us. He kept us out of trouble and on the right path."

C H A P T E R   E L E V E N

We arrive back at the house and panic ensues. The girls have returned with my mother, who is sitting on the den sofa with an ice pack on her head and her cup of wine beside her on the end table. My father sits on the other end of the sofa, while Clare stands at the kitchen door watching my mother, like a mother watching a young pup.

"Clare, what happened?"

"Your mother slipped coming into the house and hit her head on the doorframe."

"Did she fall?"

"No, she just slipped, but I saw her head hit the doorframe."

From the den, I hear my father say something. My mother choosing this moment to be stubborn, yells, "Come hell or high water, I am not going to the hospital."

I lower my head and rub my forehead. I go into the den and say, "Dad, she may have internal bleeding. You should at least go and see if she can get a CT scan."

He does not say anything. Instead, he throws his arms up in frustration and goes into the kitchen and begins sweeping the floor. This, his usual escape when moments with my mother get too tense.

Clare, the only person my mother will listen to, goes into the den and reexamines the bruise forming on her head.

"Francis, do you feel any confusion or trouble with your balance?"

In the kitchen with my father, I mutter, "That's a loaded question. She has been having trouble with confusion and balance for the past five years. Why the hell do you think we are here?"

My mother replies, "No, but I do have a little ringing in my ears. Of course, that's probably the tinnitus I have had for years."

I glance around the corner and watch Clare pull back my mother's thin gray hair. "Does this hurt?"

"Just a little."

Clare stops and kneels. She and my mother are eye to eye. "Now, do you think you lost consciousness?"

My mother gives blank look and replies, "No. I am pretty sure I did not."

I look at the three girls. They are all holding back tears. My mother has been a challenge over the last five years, but their love for her has remained unchanged. If anything, it has grown.

Clare finishes her exam of my mother and walks over to me. We retreat into the dining room so my mother cannot hear us. From the den my mother asks, "If someone is there, I need another sip of wine."

My dad puts down his broom and obliges her.

I look at Clare and say, "What do you think?"

"Well, she probably has a slight concussion."

From the dining room I see my dad in the kitchen refilling her three-ounce cup and taking it back to her in the den. He does not say anything, but concern fills his face. When he returns to the den, I hear my mother tell him, "I am not going to the hospital."

My dad, as I always did as a child, appeases her, saying, "I understand. Let's just see what Clare says."

From the dining room I continue to watch as Mary comes into the kitchen. She takes a napkin and wipes her eyes. She walks into the dining room and asks, "Does Grammy need to go to the hospital? If so, I'll go with her. I know she will need someone to keep her company."

Clare and I smile at Mary. I look at Clare with raised eyebrows as if to say, "Well?" Clare thinks for a moment and says, "Let's just keep an eye on her for now. It looks like she just has a bad bruise, but at her age it's difficult to tell."

The next day, my mother shows no signs of change from the prior day. Clare looks her over again and says, "It still just looks like a bad bruise, but I would feel better if she went to the hospital and had a CT scan."

I wonder if I should call Dr. Pong. Before I have another thought, Clare pulls me into the other room and says, "Look, your dad is a nervous wreck. I think it's best if I take your mother to the hospital and you do something to distract your father.

Henry and I distract my father by taking him to lunch at Skin's, a landmark of Shoals set in a shabby shack in a decaying mill neighborhood, which claims to serve the world's best hot dogs.

Getting into the car, my father says, "Henry, you are going to love Skin's. Nobody cooks a hot dog like they do. Your Uncle Bull and I used to go there all the time after school."

I am relieved, because it appears this will distract my father from yesterday's events with my mother, and hopefully allow him to relax. At eighty years old, he has had plenty of his share of cardiac scares and surgeries, too. I worry that, if something happens to him, there will be no one to care for my mother.

"Have they been in business for that long?" asks Henry.

With a big grin, my father says, "Yes, and you are going to love it. It's the only place I know that cooks their hot dogs in beer."

We arrive and open the screen door at Skin's, walking in as the snap of the closing door against the frame announces our arrival. An older man appears from around the old metal cash register and asks, "How many do you want?"

We order two hot dogs each and three bottles of Coke. Like an old country store, Skin's only has bottle drinks. There is no soda fountain. A pickle jar sits by the cash register. Below the counter sits a metal stand with Lance crackers and MoonPies.

In a booth the three of us sip our Cokes and my dad "holds court." He starts by saying, "Henry, when I was five my daddy used to bring me here after mill league baseball games. Can you believe we used to get five hot dogs for just a quarter? I bet back then when there was a baseball game this place would sell four hundred hot dogs in one day. People lined the street waiting to order."

As we are eating a couple of men wearing suits and ties come in. We glance over, noting how uncharacteristic their dress is to the setting, and my father comments, "Back when I was young, no one from town came here for hot dogs. Townspeople did not interact with folks in the mill. They all wanted us to stay south of town. Nowadays, I guess that does not matter."

Behind them, a person who appears homeless comes in with a Styrofoam cup. The man behind the counter fills his cup with Coke from a bottle and hands him a hot dog. They do not exchange money and nod only a thank-you.

I smile and look around to take in the atmosphere. On the wall beside our booth, I see a picture of Jimmy Carter. He has signed it, *Skin's: best hot dogs in America.* To the right of it and above is a sign exclaiming, *No Profanity!*

When Clare and my mother arrive back from the hospital, Henry, my father, and I are back from Skin's and watching the Atlanta Braves on the television, and the girls are at the pond, fishing. Both Clare and my mother look exhausted, but relieved. They enter the den, and I ask, "Well, what's the report?"

"It took a while, but they did a CT scan. The radiologist did not see any bleeding, but he did say he saw some internal bruising. He said at her age it is hard to tell and to keep a close eye on her for the next day or so."

Before I ask another question, my mother blurts out, "It's been a long day. Can someone get me some wine?"

My father rushes to the kitchen and returns with a three-ounce plastic cup filled with white wine. My mother sits in her orange leather chair and takes a sip as Clare keeps an eye on her. *Nothing ever changes.*

Disgusted, I say, "I am going down to the pond to check on the girls." Really, I need an escape.

At the pond, the girls are excited to see me. After I explain how Grammy seems to be OK, they talk about the fish they have caught and the boys that have stopped and talked to them. I enjoy their smiles and laughter. I join in and say, "You're lucky Grammy is feeling bad. Otherwise, if she saw y'all talking to boys she would probably march down here and tell you how you have no business talking to boys."

Vivian smirks and says, "Look, Dad, one boy gave me his phone number."

As the sun begins to set, we start back to the house. At the same time, the gaggle of Canada geese visiting for the summer take off. I wonder why they leave each afternoon and where they go. I enjoy their loud honks, barks, and cackles, which remind me of Hazel's old green Chevrolet Impala with its Klaxon horn—aarougah!

I see Bobby in his yard. Before going inside, I say to the girls, "Y'all go on inside. I am going to say hello to Bobby."

I walk over to Bobby's house and share the day's events with him. His wife is a nurse, which gives me a little comfort, knowing we are leaving tomorrow.

Inside, everyone except my mother and father is upstairs in their bedroom looking at their iPhones. My mother and father are on the couch. My father sits at one end watching the History Channel. My mother is stretched across the remainder of the couch. Her feet sit in his lap as she quietly snores. I say good night to my father.

In the bedroom, I say to Clare, "Do you think they will be OK?"

"I think so. Your mother napped a little on the couch, which gave me an opportunity to talk with your dad. He knows what to look for and will take her to the hospital if he sees anything change."

When the moon rises, and it's time for bed, I walk over to the window. Clare raises her head from the pillow and asks, "What are you doing?"

"I am trying to open the window."

"Why? It's too hot. Plus, the humidity."

The window sticks. "I know. I just want to open it a little so I can hear everything outside." I jab the heel of my palm. "The damn thing is painted shut."

"Be careful, John. The last thing we need is for you to put your hand through the window."

Impatient I say, "Just let me do this. I don't know how many more times we will be back." I manage to open the window about half an inch. "Good, just enough so we can hear."

The night tunes have always put me to sleep. The tree frogs sing a chorus more beautiful than any of Handel's choruses, as the bullfrogs down by the pond croak their large throats. My eyelids get heavy. I listen to the deep hoot of a mysterious great horned owl in the distant darkness.

In the morning, Clare and I pack the car. When my mother comes downstairs, Clare assesses her. "You still have a nasty bruise, but otherwise, you seem OK."

Overhearing them as I walk by, I stop and see the purple and blue goose egg on my mother's crown through her withered gray hair.

When Clare finishes, my mother pours a cup of coffee and sits at the breakfast room table. I finish packing the car and come into the breakfast room to spend a few minutes with my mother before we leave.

I look at the dark rings under my mother's eyes and can tell she spent most of last night crying. I am not sure what it was about until she looks at me and says, "Your dad and I did a lot of talking last night. I think it is time we moved into that place in Florida."

Clare and I respond with a look of astonishment. I wonder, *Could Mom be seeing the mire of her dysfunction and finally finding an internal peace beyond the horizon of her situation?*

The kids come downstairs dressed and ready for our long drive home. My mother smiles at them and says, "Poppy and I are moving to Florida. You know how much Grammy enjoys the beach." Each child gives my mother a hug and says their goodbyes.

My father joins us at the car for his goodbyes. I look at the dark clouds beginning to form on the horizon. "Looks like y'all are going have some rain a little after we leave."

My father looks up and replies, "Yes, I just hope we don't have any storms." He reaches into his pocket and hands me a $500 check made out to the residential living facility. "This is for the deposit. Can you run this by when you are back home? I will call them, so they are expecting you."

I pat my father on the back and say, "This is a big step for y'all and will be a big change. Are you sure you are ready to leave? You have been in this house for over forty years."

My father's voice cracks as he says, "Yes, it is time."

A few hours later, we are about halfway home. Clare looks at me and says, "Do you think we should call and check on your mother?"

I call, and before my father can say hello, I hear my mother yelling, "I'm not going to that fucking place. I'm staying right here in my own damn house. You can go if you want. I don't give a shit. I'll just get a divorce!"

All I say is, "Dad, I will let you know when we are home."

At home I do not call my father. I already know. I put the check in the paper shredder. I do not know what was said or why, but I will never ask. The past has taught me that my mother's storms always occur when things seem the most content.

C H A P T E R　T W E L V E

The United States Department of Justice has served Cogniv-Pharma with a subpoena about a serious and potential criminal matter regarding the company's speaker program with physicians. When Mr. Graves approved the implementation of these programs, I raised regulatory concerns about potential kickback. No one listened. I wrote memos. No one replied. Now, Mr. Graves dismisses me. Mr. Arden dismisses me, too. What does this say about my role in the organization?

Back home, my mother sits with a significant bruise on her head, lucky it's not worse. My father, worn down, faces my mother's refusal to make any concessions or changes. I know this because he called, again, and I did not answer it. Uncharacteristic for him, he left a message.

I need a rebound, something that will validate my talent and demonstrate my worth at work and something that will take my mind off the impending disaster happening with my parents. I dig deep to reassure myself. I know this will not be a sprint. Instead, it will be a marathon, like a grueling three-set match. I will endure until the end, whether it results in exhaustion or getting fired.

Determined, I place this burden on my back, refusing to cast it aside. It fills me with anticipation and dread. I know from here forward this will be uncomfortable, and the pursuit of success will cause me to do things out of the ordinary and beyond my limits. It will challenge me to become more.

As we cross the bridge out of the neighborhood on our way to Atlanta, Georgia, and the southern regionals, I take in one last look of the ponds. *I need to bounce back after my lackluster performance at the Palmetto Championships.*

My mother's temperament and jittery voice make my pulse jump like a largemouth bass.

"John, did you remember to pack your tennis rackets?"

Annoyed I respond, "Yes, of course."

"Your water cooler?"

"Yes, Mom," I say slowly and draw out my words to demonstrate my annoyance.

"Don't get impatient with me." She reminds me, "You barely qualified this year, and you need to do better."

"I know…just." I do not finish. I know she is right. An early exit will likely cost me any college offers. I must bounce back in this tournament and come out like a tiger backed into a corner.

We arrive in Atlanta and head straight to the tournament site to see who I'll play tomorrow and at what time.

I look at the drawsheet and say, "Shit! I have to play the number five seed. This isn't fair. I drew a seeded player first round and lost in last year's tournament, too."

The fifth seed is tall, muscular, and already receiving college scholarship offers from top schools in the NCAA. His father is the tennis coach at Duke University. I don't have any such pedigree. *I need to play my best.*

My mother provides me her usual and annoying comment, "It doesn't matter what he is seeded. You have more talent. You just have to use it."

My mind anguishes at the thought of another first-round loss and the demands of my mother, always believing I had more talent than any other player. I carry it like a boulder around my neck, which grows heavier each year with feelings of inadequacy and self-doubt. All caused by the constant pressure to win.

The next day, my mother drives to the tournament site in silence. I sense she is listening to her own thoughts. I grow nervous as I watch her fast and abrupt motions. At the tournament site, I trip getting out of the car. My stiff body feels like a crumbled carpet left out in the rain as I walk to report in for the match.

The match begins at noon and Atlanta has always seemed to exist as one of the hottest places on earth. On the court, during the warm-up my body eases as I begin hitting the ball. Everything begins to feel natural, and I convince myself I have nothing to lose. During warm-up, I also process my opponent's strengths and weaknesses. He is taller and stronger. His shots, especially his serve, are powerful. He is a serve-and-volleyer.

Instead of powerful topspin ground strokes, I simplify and shorten my swing. This allows me to absorb the power of my opponent's shots. I move in to hit the ball early and utilize my slice backhand to keep the ball low and out of my opponent's power zone. Many times, during the first set, my opponent struggles with this tactic. It forces him low and causes him to return shots near his feet. As a result, he pops the ball up, which sets me up to utilize my strong ground strokes to make passing shots.

We go back and forth like this each game through many deuce/ ad duels. Finally, at 5–4 I have set point. My opponent hits a twist serve that takes me to the far left. It bounces high to my backhand and I manage an awkward, but effective, chip return. Rushing the net, my opponent gets caught between hitting my return in the air or letting it bounce. He stretches for a volley and hits the ball into the net. I win the first set 6–4 and begin feeling excited about pulling off a great upset.

In the second set, the sun is high and sweat flies from our bodies at each shot. We battle back and forth. I continue to absorb his power, but his serve appears to be getting stronger as he begins to rack up service aces. Still, I stick to my strategy, until my opponent decides to change. He stops his serve-and-volley game and begins staying at the baseline. This results in long intense rallies. The long points coupled with his power begin to wear me down.

By 4–4 in the second set, we are at the two-hour mark. I go into my routine to serve. A double fault puts me down 30–40. The next point, I surprise my opponent by serving and rushing the net. He returns my serve, and I hit a perfect volley to his backhand. He scrambles and attempts a lob, which floats up for an easy overhead smash. In my excitement for such an easy winner, I swing too soon. The ball goes oo the frame of my racket and out. My mother throws down her can of Coke in disgust and I bury my face in my hands. It's happening.

Unable to recover, I lose the next several points and the second set. Exhausted from the heat and mental pressure, I easily let go of the third set and the match. I shake my opponent's hand, and he says, "You are a hell of a player. You got what it takes." I say nothing.

During the ride back to the hotel innate guilt grows from the stillness and silence. As my mother pulls into the parking lot I ask, "Do you mind if I call my girlfriend when we get back to the room?" We had not been dating long and I wanted to tell her how the match had been. Talking to her always made me feel better. She was so different than my mother. Calm, supportive.

My mother frowns at me and replies, "Yes, especially since you played like a poor lovesick puppy missing his girlfriend."

Her comment disgusts me. I wait until she leaves the room and first call my father. After giving him a summary of the match, I say, "Dad, why does Mom say these things? It's like no matter what I am not good enough."

"John," heaves my father, "it's just easier if you go along with it. She just wants what is best for you. Is there anything wrong with that? Is there anything wrong with her not wanting you to go through the pain she has lived?"

"What pain? She never tells me anything except how her daddy died while she was teaching one day, and she heard the ambulance go past the school."

My father replies, "Son, you just won't understand. No sense in trying."

I know my mother cares for me. And I know she loves me. But I do not understand why and how my life became hers, too. I say to my father, "I guess so," and we hang up.

I call my girlfriend, Hannah. I hate myself for calling her, because it seems to justify my mother's comment that I'm a lovesick puppy, but I need to hear a softer voice from another world.

I began dating Hannah in December. She was a member of the town's Cotillion club and girls in the club got to call on the boy they desired as an escort to the Christmas dance. Hannah invited me and I gladly accepted.

A week before the dance, she invited me to dinner with her family. Her mother prepared an extravagant dinner and later Hannah and I watched a movie together in the basement family area. Hannah always held herself with a degree of confidence I was incapable of displaying. Her words and body language were direct, but her tone and figure were always delicate and soft.

While we watched the movie, Hannah's floral, spicy perfume invited me closer, and we spent the second half of the movie cuddled together on the couch. Her touch reached my emotions and nurtured me far beyond the rigid, uncomfortable abrasiveness of my family.

At the dance Hannah's sexy nature was complimented by her short, but elegant black dress. We spent the night dancing together and laughing as we embraced. Afterward and for the next several weeks I frequented Hannah's house for dinner or to watch a movie. When we were not together, we spent hours on the phone.

Eventually, when my mother's defensive ire raised, she asked, "Why do you spend so much time at Hannah's house? What do they have that makes them so much better than us? Why do you like them more?"

"Nothing, Mom. I just like spending time with her."

"Well, this better not become a distraction. I don't see why you like being over there so much." In my mother's eyes, anything taking me away from the tennis court was a distraction. As a result, she did not approve of the attention I was receiving from Hannah and the attention I was giving Hannah in return.

Hannah's house was near the Cardinal Racquet Club. To spend time with her without my mother knowing, I began leaving our house early for tennis matches. This usually gave us an hour or so together. My mother got suspicious and there were many close calls. Each one brought Hannah and me closer together in some mysterious, rebellious way.

One day, I did not realize my mother had left behind me and followed me to Hannah's house. She arrived right as I was walking up Hannah's driveway and began yelling from the street, "See! I knew I couldn't trust you!"

"But, Mom," I appealed, as I saw Hannah slip back into the house. "I have not done anything. I just stopped here on my way to the tennis court."

My mother flared her nostrils. Her face reddened. "I don't care. You never told me you were coming here. You lied to me! You said you were going to the tennis court."

I hunched my shoulders and pleaded in defeat, "I am going to the tennis court."

My mother narrowed her eyes and said, "You better get your ass to the tennis court this instant and stop this nonsense now. I will deal with you when you get home."

Guilt tightened the lump in my throat. I felt weak and embarrassed. Worse, I knew that evening would be the soonest I could call Hannah to explain. That was if my mother allowed me to use the telephone.

When I finally recovered from a night of yelling, I called Hannah and explained. She comforted me by saying, "Your mother is such a hard-ass."

My voice weakened as I replied, "Yes, at least this time all I have to do is log my car mileage in a notebook the next ten days to show her where I have gone."

A few months later Hannah stopped by the Cardinal Racquet Club to watch me in a practice match. Afterwards, Hannah asked, "Why do you get so angry playing tennis?"

I avoided making eye contact, gazed downward at the car floorboard, and stammered, "I don't know."

I wish I knew, but even in one-sided wins there were moments of annoyance that I couldn't control. It was an overwhelming bad humor, which has grown since my first tennis tournament, which pulled me places I did not want to go.

I'll never forget how Hannah kissed me that day. It was different. At the time, I did not realize that it would be our last kiss. Weeks before, I had felt our relationship on the downward curve of romance. However, I did not understand until years later why it was our last kiss. She never told me, but I know it was because of the anger and conflict tennis created within me.

Like the Palmetto Championships, the southern regional is a double elimination tournament. Each player begins the tournament in the main draw, but after a player loses their first match, they are placed in the consolation round. The consolation round works by requiring participants to play two matches a day, usually early morning and then mid- to late afternoon. This means little rest, playing during the hottest portion of the day, and most of the time playing a loser from the main draw who has been only playing one match a day. Nevertheless, I win my first three matches in the consolation round with ease.

By my fourth match, exhaustion begins to set in. I am paired against an opponent who beat me a few years earlier. I remember it well, because it was a first-round tournament loss and my mother accused me of acting cocky and arrogant, which caused me to lose. These memories feed my desire for revenge.

During our warm-up, my intensity grows. I consciously stand tall, hit the ball hard with lots of topspin, and do everything I know to intimidate my opponent. I win the first set 6–2 but begin to realize my intensity has exhausted a lot of energy. This takes a toll during the second set, but I continue to fight.

In the middle of the second set at 3–3, I hit a winner. My opponent looks at me and yells, "I cannot believe this loser is even on the court with me." His tactic works because it makes me start talking to myself. *Who does this guy think he is? What a jerk.* Distracted, I lose the second set, 6–3.

I take advantage of the break between sets to refill my cooler with ice and water. As I walk back to the court, my mother stops me. I see her biting the inside of her cheek. She is breathing so hard I hear it through her nostrils. She gives me a hard smile and says, "I do not care what you have to do, but I want you to beat this asshole."

As usual, my opponent becomes my mother's opponent, too. Only winning will provide self-worth, as losing will be failure.

My mother's demand opens the gate for a wild third set, which involves more bantering with my opponent than rallies from the baseline. I draw first blood on the initial point by hitting a slice serve out wide for an ace. Rather than turn around and prepare for the next point, I continue walking toward the net. At the net I stop and stare down my opponent.

This only raises the stakes with my opponent. I am up 2–0 and he yells, "This guy is just a big sissy." His remark brings back memories of how my brother taunted me during practice matches, but I hold my emotions together.

In the third game, I hit a decent approach shot and rush the net. Somehow my opponent hits a lob over my head. I race back for it. It sails beyond the baseline, and I call it out. My opponent yells, "What the hell! The ball was clearly inside the line."

I turn toward him and reply with a scowl, "No, it was long."

"It wasn't, you piece of shit," replies my opponent as he walks toward me and slams his racket on the net. Next, he asks, "Show me the mark where it hit?"

My patience thin, I reply, "You did not hit it hard enough to make a mark. This is a hard court, not clay."

My opponent stays at the net and yells, "Whatever!"

I stand and stare at him for a moment but do not say a word. When he does not move, I get ready to serve. I go through my routine of bouncing the ball and when I look up to serve, he is still standing at the net. Intentionally acting like a smart-ass, I ask, "Is that where you intend to receive my serve?"

My opponent throws down his racket and yells, "You are nothing but a fucking cheater," as he walks off the court to ask for a line judge.

I wait for my opponent and the line judge to return. I look at my mother. She gives me a savage smile and nods her head in approval. As I walk toward her, she says, "Don't take any more shit from this guy." In the meantime, while I wait, I imagine myself hitting my opponent in the face with my fist. The image makes me feel good.

The line judge arrives, and we continue the match. At 3–2 my opponent hits a fierce serve down the middle. Tired, I do not react. However, I call it out. My opponent throws up his arms and asks the line judge, "Was that out?"

With no emotion she replies, "Yes, it was long."

This brief interaction gives me confidence. In the past year I had started wearing eyeglasses, which at times caused me to doubt myself when making calls. I go on to win the next point and move ahead 4–2.

During the changeover, my opponent intentionally mutters things so I can hear him. "Fucking four-eyed bastard." This arouses my anger, but I tell myself, *Keep it together. Four good serves and you will be up 5–2.*

Keeping my emotions together, I win the next three points. At the end of each point my opponent throws a tantrum filled with insults launched toward me. I look at the line judge as if to say, "Why are you letting this guy act this way?" She remains emotionless.

I hit a service ace down the middle of the court. My opponent just stands there. As I began to walk over to change sides he says, "What the hell are you doing? Your serve was out."

"What!" I yell back in disbelief. "That was clearly inside the line."

We approach the net and if the line judge had not been there, I think we would have started a fistfight. We stand at the net eyeing each other when the line judge says, "The serve was in. The score is 5–2. Now, please change sides of the court."

Making sure I get the last word, I look at my opponent and say, "Who's the fucking cheater now, asshole."

The line judge penalizes me a point for my verbal attack. It does not matter. Confident, I win the next game and the match. My opponent barely shakes my hand, and I do not care. I walk off the court as quickly as possible to avoid any other possible altercations. I am relieved at winning, but ashamed of my behavior.

During the ride to the hotel my legs began cramping, a bad omen for the following day. Regardless, I began rehydrating myself as my mother drives the car and says, "I am proud of you for telling that guy to fuck off." This is the first time I have ever heard my mother use the f-bomb. We laugh like idiots as she pulls into the hotel.

The following morning my eyelids sag with sleepiness. Each limb attached to my body aches with heaviness. Drunk with fatigue, I manage to roll out of the bed and begin thinking about the morning's match. I am playing someone I beat last fall at the southern indoor. However, the voice in my mind reminds me this match will not be in the comfort of faster indoor courts, which complement my power and aggression.

At the tennis center, my mother reminds me, "John, win both matches today and you will qualify for the nationals."

National tournaments, except for one early in my career, have existed only as a dream. I have never been this close to qualifying.

On the court, my body is stiff and sluggish, and I struggle early in the match. The Atlanta sun rises, and I feel the heat and humidity sucking at my energy. I lose the first set.

During the changeover I take extra time to clear my mind. I pour ice water on my towel and place it on the nape of my neck. This gives me an injection of strength and rejuvenation. I win the next four games. My opponent does not crack. Steady, he fights back, but I eventually win the second set 6–3.

At the beginning of the third set I hope for another fast start. I put all my energy into the next five games. My opponent matches my energy, and the score is 2–3 when I start feeling my body begin to break down. Mentally, I am done, which means emotionally I am done, too.

The score is deuce. We are both two points from winning the next game. I know losing my serve and going down 2–4, will mean an uphill comeback. I feel powerless but go into my routine of bouncing the ball in preparation to serve. My first serve goes long. As I begin to bounce the ball for my second serve, I feel my muscles tense. I take a little extra time. *Just get it over the net*, I say to myself. My second serve hits the net. Double fault. My anger and rage from the first set returns and I throw down my racket and yell.

As I pick up my racket I hear a tournament umpire yell, "Point penalty!"

Sweat flies from my head when I spin around and reply, "Point penalty? I never got a warning." The standard penalties for a player were receiving a warning before a point penalty.

"Yes, you did," replies the stout woman as she walks toward the fence surrounding the court. "I gave you a warning in the first set."

"No, you didn't." I reply, challenging her. "I never heard you."

She sharpens her voice and says, "It does not matter."

At this point, I lose my mind and begin yelling back, "How can you give someone a warning when they do not acknowledge it? I never heard you give me a warning. How can you do this to me?"

The umpire is at the fence, her fingers clenching the chain links, "Listen here!"

"John, shut up and start playing," my mother yells to interrupt.

This stops me, but it is too late. The little fight remaining in my body focuses itself on the perceived unfairness. Down 2–4, I lose the next eight points and the match. As we shake hands my opponent says, "Don't worry about it, man. If it helps, I didn't hear her give you a warning, either."

Devastated, I sit with my face in my towel, holding back tears. I bemoan that this is the closest I have ever been to qualifying for nationals and this is how it ends. I eventually walk off the court. My mother stands waiting for me. I see the disappointment and anger in her face, but I do not care. I just want to go home.

Back home the adults I practice with ask, "How did you do at the southerns?"

I reply, "I finished in the top forty-eight." But before I have time to explain that it is my best finish ever, a follow-up question is directed at me.

"Did you qualify for nationals?"

"No."

"Well, that's OK."

Like always, my performance is good, but never good enough. This eats at me. I have the talent to rip a winner from anywhere on the court, sometimes even when I'm out of position. Tennis is automatic, robotic, but no one explains execution.

I suffer in silence. Still, I know finishing in the top forty-eight gets me much closer to my goal of a tennis scholarship.

Before leaving my house for work I sense my back is against the wall. As I stand by my car, putting my computer and files in the backseat, I notice iridescent gray dragonflies hovering over the hood, softly buzzing their transparent wings. Before opening the car door, I reflect on the last two days. It's difficult to silence my mother's voice and the memoires from my youth. "John has so much talent, he does not know what to do with all of it," and, "John just never plays up to his talent." I see angry glares of disappointment. I feel the same numbness, like a patient etherized on the table.

Later in the afternoon, I open an email from a news service, and I am greeted by the following headlines: *Miami Drug Company to Pay $900 Million to Settle Allegations It Paid Doctors Kickbacks to Prescribe Memory Drug.*

I open the article and read it.

Reading the article fills me with a sense of self-worth and a feeling of validation. I bear no ill will toward Cogniv-Pharma; however, the recent settlement lifts the shadow of doubt that has been hanging over my head like a dark cloud.

The entire day, I feel energized. I research everything I can find about the matter in Miami, including the corporate integrity agreement executed as part of the settlement. Confident I understand the facts and circumstances of the case, I go over to the C-suite to Mr. Graves's office. Still, my hands shake as I knock on the suite door. I approach his assistant and say, "Good afternoon, I am sorry to interrupt but it is important I see Mr. Graves."

His assistant takes a quick look at Mr. Graves's calendar. "OK, he appears to be free for the next few minutes and is not on the phone. Let me ask if he will see you."

As I wait for his assistant, I rub my sweaty palms against my pants. Anxiety absorbs my energy as I listen to their muted conversation. His assistant finally opens the door as I hear Mr. Graves say, "Whatever."

His assistant walks out, followed by Mr. Graves holding his suit jacket. "What's on your mind, John? I only have a few minutes."

I reply, "I am terribly sorry to interrupt your day, but I have been studying the recent settlement out of Miami. It appears to be the same type of speaker program we have engaged physicians in regarding RemMem."

Mr. Graves clears his throat and patronizes me saying, "I seriously doubt they are the same. Anyway, you know how things are in Miami. It's a different world down there. Those people in South Florida are different."

I attempt to avoid sounding equally patronizing and say, "I am not familiar with Miami; however, the settlement release makes it appear the Miami office is working with the Middle District of Florida, where Cogniv-Pharma exists. So, I am sure our subpoena is part of a broad effort and not a single inquiry."

There is a brief pause. Mr. Graves sighs. "OK, John." The tone of his voice reminds me who is the superior. "What do you propose?"

I feel like a child again in front of my mother. "Nothing, sir. I just thought you may be interested in hearing this." As with my mother, I quickly change the subject and say, "Also, I know you keep all the minutes from the board of director meetings in your office. I need to make copies of certain meetings, as it relates to the subpoena."

Mr. Graves rolls his eyes. "John, I am leaving for a dinner event, and we are closing the office for the day. Help yourself to the minutes. They are in the bound books stacked on top of the file cabinet. But just remember, I plan to fight this subpoena in court before complying with it."

They leave and I hurry to make the necessary copies of the minutes I need. I do not need to review them. I know the general counsel is too experienced and only includes the bare minimum in terms of describing procedures and votes. As I place the last book on the file cabinet, I look at my iPhone and see an email from Dr. Pong.

John, good to talk with you the other day. I finished reviewing the studies. Each study shows minimal evidence of

*postsurgical complications, except the studies led by the physi-
cians on the list you showed me the other day. The studies led by
those physicians document no signs of postsurgical complications.
Even more interesting, the total number of patients in studies
conducted by the physicians on your list is 20 times more than
the patients in studies by other physicians.*

*I have searched for additional records and found nothing
more. This does not make sense, so I even called a medical
school classmate who participated in the study. She was not on
your list. However, she made a strange comment. Something
about an offer to receive additional payments from Mr. Graves
through what sounded like a foundation. She would not share
anything else. She said, "Cogniv-Pharma is too powerful, and
I am not going to get tangled up with them."*

I read the email twice. Another win. My conscience weighs
heavy regarding what I must do next, because my mind tells me to
do something unusual and uncharacteristic for an ethics officer.

I close the door to Mr. Graves's office and lock it. One by
one, I open each desk drawer, making sure to be steady and not
disrupt anything. I do the same with the file cabinet. I find only a
few documents related to RemMem, but nothing relatable to the
subpoena or the email from Dr. Pong.

After I close the last file drawer, I grab the copies I had made
and slowly unlock and open the office door. I am relieved no one has
entered the office suite. I think, *Surely, I would have been fired and
humiliated.* Still, I am perplexed. There must be records somewhere.
My mind floods with caution. *Is this worth it? To what lengths am I
willing to risk everything I have worked for?*

I leave and head to my car excited to go home and tell Clare
about my day. There is more and the challenge to discover it rouses a
competitive side of myself I have buried since playing tennis.

Inside the car, I place the copies in my work bag, and head out
of the garage when Dr. Pong calls me.

"Hey, John, did you get my email?"

I reply, "Yes, I did. Obviously, there is more to this. I knew it. There had to be." Dr. Pong concurs, and I continue, "When I saw your email I was alone in Mr. Graves's office. He gave me permission to go in and copy minutes from the board book. While I was there, I quickly peeked through his files but did not find anything."

"John," Dr. Pong's voice of caution challenges me, "you shouldn't do that. What if you got caught?"

"I know. It's just I am over being dismissed about this like a child asking permission from his mother." I can feel myself getting angrier, feeling exactly as I did as a teenager. I clear my throat. "Anyway, did your medical school classmate give you a name or anything that may identify the foundation she mentioned?"

"No, but she sounded really weird and out of character. She said the name of the foundation was secret."

"Secret," I shout, the anger back. "Foundations must be organized and filed with the IRS. How can they be secret?"

There is a pause, and I ask, "Can you give me this physician's number and let me call her?" Before Dr. Pong can answer I say, "No, hold on a minute. That could get back to Graves and tip him off."

"Yes, I was just about to say that." Dr. Pong gives a thoughtful "Hmm" and says, "Graves keeps records of everything, especially when it involves money. He is a smart man. Clandestine, too. My guess is, if he does have documents about this, they are either at his home or locked in a safe-deposit box at a bank."

"I suspect you're right. Anyway, thanks for the information. I almost have everything ready to send in response to the subpoena." I do not share with Dr. Pong that my mind is racing for ideas of how to search inside Mr. Graves's house.

"Glad I helped, but I don't think I really gave you any helpful information."

"You did," I reply. "This thing just seems to have lots of layers to peel back."

I hang up the call and tap my fingers on the steering wheel while I wait for the light to change when suddenly I remember that in a few weeks Mr. Graves will host his end of spring party before staff and board members begin to leave for their summer family vacations. This year the party is at his house.

C H A P T E R   T H I R T E E N

In the car, I select Robert Johnson on my playlist. The day, deep and intense, makes me feel like a hellhound is on my trail. After so many years of hard work and overcoming lots of adversity, I wonder if my fortitude to discover the truth will mean making a deal with the Devil.

When I was young, tennis attracted me to the emotional dirge of the blues. Its visceral and raw sounds with simple syncopated rift patterns called to my heart. I related to the emotional intensity and the troubled stories about loss and depression—a brutal, but honest recognition of what I thought of my own reality. It filled a space in my soul that longed for an intense connection.

Regardless, and against all my efforts, life was tennis. Although I did not understand or respect it, people in town defined me as a tennis player. Everything else was secondary.

As my enjoyment of the blues grew, the ghostly whispers of blues legends and the songs of the old Mississippi Delta blues singers like Robert Johnson beckoned me to try. I grew a strong desire to play the distinctive sounds of sliding a piece of metal across the fingerboard.

My mother holds on to everything. She never throws out boxes of the check copies from the bank; they line the den cabinets. She fills other cabinets with fabric samples and remnants that might be of use one day. The back room to the garage is filled with furniture she intends to refinish. My family holds on to things forever. Closets explode with items of no value.

In one hall closet, for as long as I can remember, sits an old acoustic guitar. I've never seen anyone take it out and it does not appear unique in any way.

I ask my mother, "Whose old guitar is that in the hall closet?"

"That was my father's."

I wince because I know anything holding the spirit of my grandfather haunts my mother's being. Regardless, I continue, "Do you mind if I have it?"

"Sure," responds my mother with no thought or comment.

Upstairs in my room with the guitar I wear a wide grin, but I also am aware of how the guitar will ignite my mother's memory of her father. I do not understand their dynamic, but I know his memory haunts her every day.

Back in my teen years, I spent days in my room with my grandfather's guitar and my stereo, trying to imitate the eerie sounds of Robert Johnson. I spent hours in my room trying to hone my skills. I plied my craft slowly, as the hardships of tennis inspired my individual sound and personal experience of blues: loneliness, hardship, and living on the road. The sounds evoked the mysticism of the American South. I fell in love with the legends. To me, they were filled with a monumental mystery too tempting to not be considered truth. It felt etched in the darkest pages of history.

After a week with the guitar, I am back at work preparing for the southern open tournament in Jackson, Mississippi. After a strong showing at the southern indoor and now my best finish at the southern regionals, top forty-eight, I keep reminding myself, my mother's expectations are high. However, the southern open is a clay court tournament, my least favorite surface. Clay courts do not complement my game. Their abrasive surface absorbs the ball's speed, taking away the strength of my power. Points last longer, there are fewer winners, and footing is always a challenge. Most of all, winning on clay courts requires strategy.

The southern open is one of only two clay court tournaments I play each year. This means extra practice time at the Cardinal Racquet Club. Typically, a practice match in the morning and another in the afternoon.

During a week of intense preparation, I am in the middle of a practice match with a middle-aged club member I know well. The court is on the near side of the road going by the club. During the middle of a point, I see a Honda Accord pull over into the grass and a high school friend, Ellie, gets out of the car and walks over to the fence.

Ellie, a cheerleader, is a girl who never seems to date anyone, but every guy, including me, dreams of having a shot with her. I had not come close to dating anyone since Hannah. My mother would have lost it, and I was embarrassed about my behavior at the tournament Hannah witnessed and did not want others to see that side of me.

Ellie, though, is different. She has endless long, tan legs. She is athletic, too, with a firm body, and she always wears her hair in a ponytail. Like most of my friends, she has never seen me play tennis. She stands at the fence and watches until it is time for a changeover. As I change sides, she gives me a sly grin and an animated, "Hi, John."

My dimples blossom red as I go over and reply, "Hi, what are you up to?"

She gives her head a flirtatious tilt and says, "Oh, nothing. I was just driving by and saw you playing tennis. I thought I would stop and say hello."

My emotions feel raw. I do not know what to say other than, "How's your summer?"

"It's good," she replies and then blurts, "Some of us are going out to Lake Hartwell tomorrow to ride Jet Skis. Want to come along?"

I look down at the court and notice the uneven vinyl line near the net. Without looking at her I say, "No, I've got to get ready for a tournament next week."

Her brightness appears to dim as she leaves saying, "OK, call me if you change your mind."

Before we continue our match, the friend I am playing looks at me with a crinkled brow and says, "You must be crazy. Do you understand what you just did? Nobody rides down this road except to come to the tennis courts. She clearly likes you and wants you to go to the lake with her."

"I know. It's just too complicated."

None of my friends understand. My mother views Lake Hartwell as a place with no adult supervision. A place where teenagers get in trouble. Without asking, I already know her response: *Absolutely not. The lake is where teenagers drink and get in trouble. Worse, you could injure yourself.*

Still, in my mind I want to reply, *Yes, teenagers go to the lake to do what teenagers do. Drink beer and try to act on their sexual thoughts and emotions. Get a grip, Mom.* I don't, obviously.

The remainder of the match all I think about is Ellie. I imagine her tan trim stomach in a bikini that barely rises to her lower hips. Her hair pinned in a simple ponytail that sways with her hips as she strides with her long, slender legs. God, how I desire to just touch her bare skin.

What a dope, I think. I'd rather bust my ass on the tennis court all day instead of rubbing suntan oil on Ellie, or, better, her rubbing it on me.

After traveling through sheets of rain through the tornado alley of the Mississippi Valley, we reach Jackson, Mississippi. In the hotel room I unpack my tennis rackets. Beside them I lean the guitar against the wall.

I open the tenth-floor curtains and see the modern skyline of Jackson, the "city with soul," through the haze and humidity. I close my eyes and think about Jackon's turbulent history and remember how this slogan also acknowledges the city's oppressive past.

I know the sole purpose of our trip is tennis, but I could not resist packing the guitar. After all, Mississippi does not inspire tennis.

The cotton fields, railroads, and slaughterhouses that surround the Delta only inspire the blues. The tournament will be close enough to visit Clarksdale. I long to sit at the corner of Routes 49 and 61 at midnight to see if the Devil appears. I've got the crossroad blues and Imma sinkin' down.

When we arrive at the country club, I do not sever my soulful connection to the blues. I do not want to lose it. At the club I see many familiar faces from years of tennis. My mother shares with the other mothers my summer wins and losses. I know that once we are alone, my mother will turn these conversations into unattainable expectations for tomorrow's tournament. She will make two- and three-degree connections of who I have beaten and who the competitors I have beaten have beaten until she has me having an indirect win over everyone in the tournament. Also, like always, she will insist on how I am more than capable of beating everyone.

After leaving the tournament site, we drive into downtown Jackson and stop at Smith Park. There is little to see. Massive trees surround grassy green spaces and rolling hills. A performing stage stands empty. I imagine myself on it with my guitar. Behind it I see a large homeless man peeing. The image cuts deep and I feel helpless, a feeling I do not like.

After the park, we drive to nearby Ridgeland to the Northpark Mall. As always, we split up and go shopping, or mostly looking. I explore Waldenbooks and go to the center of the mall, where the streaming sounds of a hollow electric guitar flow through the high atrium. The "fat" tones call me, and I listen, mesmerized by the complement of the drummer painting expressive sounds with brushes as the bass guitarist rhythmically connects the threesome in a deep bluesy character.

I lose track of time, but it does not matter. My mother passes by and stops. Together we listen. The music, unlike tennis, connects us.

I watch my mother. The music seems to take away her worry and agitation. No longer rigid, my mother appears beautiful. She turns to me and says, "Don't you just love it here? Everywhere you go people are playing such cool music."

"Yes, Mom," I reply, "that's why I brought the guitar. I want to learn how to play these sounds. I love it so much."

I suspect commenting about the guitar is what makes her face tighten and causes her rigidity to return, because she replies, "John, we need to get back to the hotel. You have a match tomorrow and we need to focus on why we are here."

It is only 8:00 the next morning and the humidity hits me in the face like a heavy, wet sponge. I win my first match, although the uncertain footing of clay and the long points under the pounding sun made it a long match. My next match is against an opponent I beat last winter at the southern indoor. However, clay courts do not suit my game. After beating him 6–2, 6–2 on indoor courts, I lose 3–6, 4–6. I do not throw a tantrum or my racket. I knew from the beginning of the match this was not my day; I was going to lose.

After the match I see my mother's stiff posture as she stands by the car. She does not say anything as we begin to drive away. Noticing we are taking a different route I ask, "Mom, where are we going?"

"There are some mill outlets nearby. A lot of times these mills make Polo and Izod clothes and sell the defects at their outlets for nearly nothing."

"Defects, what do you mean?"

"Oh, don't worry about it. No one can tell. I am sure a lot of those expensive clothes the wealthy families back home living in Windsor Hall wear come from these outlets. Even they cannot afford all the name brands they wear."

Windsor Hall is the extravagant neighborhood in the town of Shoals where all the doctors reside. It is a neighborhood my mother has always longed to live in. I have always found it curious that, in a neighborhood filled with doctors, the grandest, most opulent home belongs not to one of them, but to the man who runs the town's funeral home.

Always comparing us and herself to others, my mother drives to the outskirts of town. Like back home, lush green yards and stately homes transition to falling clapboard houses and scrub yards as we drive into the mill village.

The mill looks like Shoals Mill, too. It stands as a massive three-story brick building with tall windows. The parts of the building not in use are beginning to crumble. What was not crumbling had been painted with graffiti like the abandoned boxcars by the railroad track.

We walk into the mill outlet. Tables stand in a large room. Each has a sign noting the size of the clothing articles on top. I look down at the scratched dark wood floors and wonder how they looked when the room contained spinning looms with cotton dust floating in the air. The wood floors also remind me how state laws in the South prohibited Black men from working mill jobs, other than in the freight yard and sweeping the floors of lint and dried tobacco spit.

The workers and shoppers are a homogenous group: dirty shoes, shirts with a missing button, and unkempt hair. They speak with a broken version of "twangy" English, some with slow drawls. Everyone looks like a resident of Shoals Mill.

This appearance does not deter my mother. She browses tables and racks and finally appears at the cash register, where I am waiting in a chair. "Look," she gleefully says holding a pile of Polo shirts. "I told you this is where they buy all these name brands."

I give a puzzled look and say, "But why are the inside tags cut in half?"

"That's what they do with the defected ones."

Back in the hotel room my mother asks, "Do you want to ride up to the tournament and see who you play tomorrow morning?"

"Not really," I reply with hesitation. "I'd rather stay inside," I say as I pick up my guitar and begin tuning it.

My mother glares at me and says, "We are not here for you to play that damn guitar. You can stay here, but I am going to look at the tournament draw. I suggest you put that thing up and begin thinking about your match tomorrow."

I know what this means, so I lean the guitar against the wall. My renewed spirit now broken, I reply, "Yes, ma'am, I'm coming."

At the tournament site, my mother stands with me looking at the drawsheet. She finds my opponent and says, "Look here, this is who you are playing tomorrow. He lost 6–1, 6–0 to a guy you beat earlier this year. And look at the other players who will likely fall into your bracket. You have beaten them or have beaten someone who has beaten them."

My mother's expectations, like the heat and humidity, are unbearable. My mind is crying, and the heat is going to kill me and my game.

And it finally does.

During the next match, the humidity seems to hold my shots in the air. The sauna-like atmosphere is heavy. It makes everything feel thicker, my racket and especially the balls, which by the end of the first two games have absorbed so much water they fluff up, making them slower. My opponent reaches my best shots and returns them high with lots of topspin. Each rally seems longer than the next. Finally, cramps begin and my body malfunctions.

I want to quit, but I look over at my mother. She has moved from sitting in the bleachers to standing by the courtside fence with crossed arms. I play on and at one point my mother claps her fingers through the fence like she wants to shake it. I hear her loud silent moans of disgust. They are the only thing that seems to distract me from the cramps in my hand.

I lose, finishing the tournament in the bottom one hundred. A far cry from my finish at the southern regionals. Worse, by the time I lose the final point, my mother has already walked to the car, cranked it, and is waiting.

I arrive at the car. My mother is sullen and withdrawn. She wears a long look of suffering, which tells me she is pissed. She howls at me, "You are nothing but a jack-of-all-trades and a master of none. You will never understand what you have." My heavy heart sinks. I have let her down, again.

As we turn onto the on-ramp for Interstate 20, she explodes. Tears, like the rain when we arrived in Jackson, stream down her face.

She yells about lack of effort, not caring about tennis, and wasting my talent. "You and that ridiculous damn guitar. God has given you all this talent and wasting it like you did today is a sin. He should have given it to someone who appreciates it."

Her words fall down on me like hail and raise questions. How am I committing a sin by losing? Am I going to end up in hell?

She continues to yell about the guitar, saying, "You let that guitar ruin a perfect opportunity for a strong end of the year ranking and, more importantly, a scholarship opportunity."

Confused, I know not to speak. We haven't spoken about the Citadel in a while and I'm not going to start now. Instead, I look back, expecting to see a hellhound on my trail.

She continues, "You had no business bringing that damn guitar and we sure as hell aren't going to some damn museum in Clarksdale." She stomps on the accelerator and shouts, "We are going home!" The car lunges forward as I fall back in my seat. Without notice, the car begins to jerk and sputter. I see steam rising from the hood as my mother pulls onto the exit ramp and into the closest service station. She busted a hose.

Silence surrounds us as we wait at the service station. I know better than to fuss or comment about the car. Instead, I use the few dollars I have in my pocket to play the Donkey Kong machine, while my mother sits and sulks after calling my father from the pay telephone.

The service station mechanic fixes the hose, and we are back on the road. This reinvigorates my mother's disgust. I do not remember when she stopped lecturing me about my performance at the tournament. I just remember everything was about wasted talent, lack of effort—and, of course, the guitar.

Back home the cooler, drier air does not lower my mother's barometric pressure. Her storm of emotion grows. While we unpack the car, she grabs the shirts she bought at the mill outlet. She balls them into a wad. "You don't deserve these, but I can't return them, so here," she says as she throws them and hits me in the face.

The tense car ride home has eroded my patience, and I retaliate saying, "Thanks, just what every teenager wants, discount defects."

My mother grabs her forehead and pulls her hair back. She points her finger at me and says, "Well, that's about how you played this week while you wasted our time together."

"Time together?" I reply. "How is going to a tennis tournament, playing in the hot sun, and then riding home to your lecturing 'spending time together'?"

As always, this attack is countered by my mother conjuring the ghosts of her past. "You will never know what it is like to live on the mill hill. Plus, you do not know what it is like to lose your father."

Tears began falling from her eyes. This calls to the guilt I hold inside. I have learned how to hold a lot in, but today I let it out. I yell back, "What am I supposed to do with that? I would think, as my mother, you would never want me to experience that. How do you think it feels to have never known my grandfather?"

My mother is shaking. She says, "You do not understand. You are my serendipity. You are everything I ever wanted. I am so disappointed with you."

Her words make me lose control. I pick up the closest thing I can find, which is the guitar, and slam it onto the driveway. The body of the guitar shatters and the force of the blow dislocates the neck from the body. I point the broken guitar, which is now only held together by the strings, with its body dangling from the neck, at my mother and shout, "What do you think about that?"

My mother runs inside howling. "That was my father's!"

Not finished, I take a tennis racket and repeat the act, smashing it against the driveway, too.

I unpack the remaining contents of the car while my mother stays in her bedroom wailing. When I hear her crying louder, I sit at the piano and play various pieces until I no longer hear her crying.

My mother never comes out of her room. Later, I eat a sandwich for dinner and wait for my father's arrival from work. He is working a late shift, and I do not expect him to be home until 9:00. I watch TV until I see his headlights flash through the den bay window as he rounds the pond for home.

My father enters the door and asks, "Where's your mom?"

"She has been in her bedroom since we returned home."

He asks, "What happened?"

I breathe in, holding back tears. My father's gentle approach melts my bitterness from the events of the day. "Mom is upset because, after we got home, we started yelling and I broke the old guitar."

"The guitar that has been sitting in the closet for years?"

"Yes, plus I broke one of my rackets, too. I'm sorry, Dad."

My dad lifts his hand as if to say, "There is no need to apologize." Next, he lets out a heavy sigh and gently shakes his head. He knows what is waiting for him upstairs.

As he turns around, I ask, "Dad, what was it like living on the mill hill?"

"What do you mean?"

"Mom always tells me how I will never know what it was like, brings it up when we're fighting badly like that, but she never actually tells me anything about it."

My father, with his noncontroversial nature, replies, "Son, it's getting late. Go to bed. We will talk about this later."

My family appreciates the convenience of forgetting. They never talk about their past. Worse, each monstrosity of an argument or fight is met the next day with the attitude that nothing happened. That is how the next day is for me. No one mentions the guitar, I buy a new racket with money from cutting the grass at the club, and we all go back to our daily lives, like yesterday was just a bad dream.

CHAPTER FOURTEEN

When I arrive home from work, I stand in the driveway and admire the sunset peering through the Spanish moss hanging on the live oaks. By the front door of the house a mockingbird sits on the wooden bench, the same bench my mother gave me to serve as a couch in my first apartment. When she brought it over, she said, "Enjoy it. This bench was expensive."

Now, it sits and rots.

On my way home, I stopped by the grocery store, so I've arrived home with an armful of grocery bags, which I place onto the counter by the stove. Clare peers into the bags and rhetorically asks, "Steak and brussels sprouts. Must have been a really bad day?"

"That's right," I rejoice as I reach for the corkscrew and a Bordeaux wine stem. "I stopped by the grocery store across town with the actual meat counter and the nice wine shop beside it."

Clare looks at the wine glass and scowls at me. "Ugh, I hate those glasses. They always break in the dishwasher. Do you have to use those?"

I raise my eyebrows and intentionally give her a condescending look as my voice changes to a solemn and intellectual reply, "My dear, wine is a serious art requiring the most delicate glass for the most critical evaluation of the wine aroma and taste. Such an intentional vessel must be cared for by hand and never a mindless machine."

I give Clare a smile and sardonic wink as I pour.

Before taking the first sip, I hold the glass in the light, slightly tilting it to examine the color. "Beautiful. Clare, have you ever considered the difference in eating grapes and drinking wine?"

Clare rolls her eyes and replies, "No, but I am sure you have." *Every day.*

I lower my glass and reply, "It is amazing how a bunch of grapes shed their initial natural shape and form, yet their juicy essence is preserved and elevated to something greater." I pause for a moment. *I wonder what else in nature, like me, is awaiting the opportunity to show its secret meaning.*

Before I continue, Clare reminds me, "John, Henry is at practice, but why don't you go into the den and say hello before you start dinner."

I go into the den. The twins and Vivian, watching television, have overheard our conversation. Katie looks up at me and asks, "Dad, aren't you going to pour Mom a glass?"

I instantly recognize the joke and reply loud enough for Clare to hear, "Your mom gave up red wine the day after our first engagement party." I yell to Clare, who overheard my comments, "Remember that night? You did not want our friends to leave so you continued to open bottles of wine."

I look at the kids and can tell they want to hear the rest—again. I give them a clever wink and continue, "I found your mom later that night propped up in her bed reading. The only problem was she did not realize she was holding the book upside down."

The four of us laugh as Clare yells from the kitchen, "Real funny. Your dad is such a comedian. But yes, that was a miserable night, and I spent most of it on the bathroom floor."

I go back into the kitchen, where Clare playfully smiles at me and gives me a kiss. "Anything I can do to help with dinner?"

"No, other than help me figure out what the kids will eat."

Clare brings me back into reality replying, "Sure. I assume *your* dinner means another stressful day."

I take a deep breath and a large sip of wine. "I shared with Mr. Graves a settlement announced by the DOJ and a Miami-based pharmaceutical company over the same speaker programs we operate with physicians. I am confident the entire state of Florida is under review, and every company doing this will have the same fate, including us."

"What did Mr. Graves say?"

"Nothing has changed. He does not care." I take another sip. "But get this. Dr. Pong called me. I think there is definitely something to the allegations about cranial surgery complications. Dr. Pong never really said, but he hinted that there may be other payments that have gone undiscovered."

Clare replies, "That is interesting. I know how much you respect Dr. Pong, and I think you need to stay close to him as you learn more about this."

"Yes, I agree. We are kindred souls."

Clare, a natural-born nurturing soul, gazes into my eyes and says, "I appreciate your thoughtfulness and the depth of your perception. There is a lot to you, and you have so much to tell."

I lower my head and say, "I know. It is what makes this so damn hard."

Clare places her hand on my shoulders and says, "Hey, look at me. Your opportunity will come. Just be patient. Put this aside for now. Henry has his spring football game on Thursday, and the girls have a birthday, too. That should give you something happy to look forward to."

I lean to give Clare a kiss, but the twins, Mary and Katie, shatter the delicate moment with their ear-piercing screeches from the den. In unison, they protest, "You mean our birthday is once again the same day as Henry's stupid football game. It's not fair. Each year, our birthday gets ignored by us all going to some stupid football game that does not even count."

It did not surprise me that my Enneagram results identified me as a peacemaker. I have been doing it all my life, ignoring pain, numbing my discomfort, and avoiding discomfort to the point of apathy. "Girls," I interject, "your brother is a senior. Please just let it go. It will be his last one."

The words hang in the air and suddenly I realize these words were my mother's demands each day during my brother's high school senior year when he wanted me to go to the tennis court with him. Each day, I loathed this duty handed out by my mother, but I complied, no matter how much it upset me.

The sky at the spring football game gives an energetic blue glow. In the distance, big puffy clouds darken and give off flashes of electricity. The heat is almost unbearable, yet there is a feeling of playfulness dancing in the air.

The teams come onto the field. Henry looks like a giant compared to most of the smaller players. Like a gladiator, he shaded his face with black paint. I appreciate his enthusiasm on the gridiron.

Weeks prior to the game, I frequently left work early, drawn like a kid to football practices. The coaches exuded energy and positive enthusiasm that I never received and that I struggled to give to my son.

I watched the pregame workouts, feeling Henry's passion seep into my weary bones. Before the team left the field for the locker room, they gathered around Henry, and he led them in a chant that stirred something deep within me.

As the game begins, Henry's enthusiasm burns bright, but he stands isolated at the far end of the sideline, away from the coaches. The coaches substitute many team members in and out of the game, but never Henry, who remains stationary. I get impatient with each passing second of the game.

After the first quarter, I walk down the steps to the first row. I holler at Henry. "Why are you not playing?"

Henry throws up his arms. I get frustrated at his response. "You're not getting in the game by standing around playing grab-ass."

He glares at me.

I emphasize my frustration by pointing to the coaches and saying, "Get your ass over there and get into the game."

"OK!" he shouts back in disgust. "What am I supposed to do? I'm trying."

I recognize his disgust.

When I return to my seat Clare glares at me and says, "What do you think you're doing? You're making this ten times worse."

I clench my jaw and say to Clare through gritted teeth, "I am just trying to motivate him to get into the damn game."

Clare shakes her head. "You're acting like your mother."

I look at Clare and then I look at the disgust on the face of my son. I think to myself, *I have become my mother.*

We ride home from the football game in silence as my anxiety fills the car with tension. I know I have created a mess, but I do not know how to fix it. Conversations are a dance that is reciprocal and complementary, but tonight, everyone is a wallflower in response to my behavior.

When we arrive home, rather than wait for Henry, who will be home later, I seek solace from the night by going out for a walk. As I walk, I listen to the night, hoping to hear God's rhythmic patterns and to find the intimate connection with nature that has always healed my soul.

Like the evening's humidity, my mind weighs heavy. I consider how my earlier behaviors were manifested out of love and my desire of wanting those I love to live their most extraordinary life possible. This longing to seize the day escaped me when I was young because I was never allowed to leave the cocoon of my parents' safety.

Most of my early years were spent articulating to my parents how no one ever emerged prepared for everything. I have always held on to the belief that a curious life is believing that flash of light that finds your mind and plucks the strings of your heart, and you follow it, knowing you have more to learn. My light was eclipsed by tennis and later stunted by memories of the past.

I pause and enjoy how the night jasmine curls along the iron fence and breathes its perfume into the air, giving it a hint of moist sweetness. Droplets of sweat dance as they gather on my forehead and prepare to run down my face.

Earning a law degree and entering a dignified profession did not provide me with immunity from the excesses of my family. *Do the traits inherited from my family live too deep in my pores to be eradicated? Are they too volatile to be capped like a well?*

I feel a thickening of sadness rising in my throat as tears form in my eyes. Like my mother, I do not want to become my past. I say to myself, *You acted no different tonight than your mother each time she came to see you play.* These words fall on me like hail, the memories too burdensome.

I return home, and, as after many walks, I have no answers, only emotions. My mind remains cluttered with charred memories. Inside the house, everything is quiet. I sit until I hear Henry come in. He notices the strained look on my face and says, "Dad, are you OK?"

"Yeah."

"Why are you still up?"

"Henry, I wanted to talk to you about something." I hesitate a minute to keep my internal sadness within and continue, "I am sorry about tonight."

Henry looks at me and says, "What do you mean?"

I give a pensive smile and say, "You know, the yelling and telling you to get your head in the game. It was not fair for me to say those things, especially in front of everyone. I promise it will never happen again." I want to say more, but I do not know how. Too much about my past seethes beneath. One day I will tell him. I will need to tell everyone.

Henry nods his head in his usual unsure way and says, "Thanks, Dad."

Before he goes to the shower I reply, "Son, I just want you to enjoy the game and your teammates. That's something I never learned."

Henry simply replies, "OK, Dad."

As he goes upstairs, I think to myself, *This time, I really mean it.*

CHAPTER FIFTEEN

A few weeks pass and Mr. Graves opens his house for the annual end of spring party. He started this ritual as a way for the executive team to gather one last time before departing for their lavish summer homes. It is no surprise the Pinnacle Club caters the party.

Mr. Graves's house is one of the largest in the gated country club community. Each house in the neighborhood is designed with the timeless proportions and symmetry that only the most skilled craftsman can create. Each house stands with an imposing appearance. European imports sit in every driveway.

Clare and I arrive, and I hand my keys to the valet. We walk to the receiving line at the front door. There, Mr. Graves and his wife greet each guest. As we approach, two large BMW SUVs arrive behind us. Each driver is a doctor named in the subpoena and is accompanied by a much younger wife. When they see each other, the wives exchange silly gestures while hugging one another, like stars on a reality television program. Mr. Graves, eager to speak with the physicians, pushes us through his greeting line, giving us a brief and simple welcome.

At the party, Clare and I mingle, making sure to speak with everyone. We listen to summer plans: trips to Europe, shows in New York City, and wine tours in Napa. When we describe our summer plans, a week at the beach and the kids going to a local church camp, the wives say, "Bless your heart. That's cute."

After we make the rounds, Clare says to me, "I am ready anytime you are."

I look around the outside veranda. At the pool, a crowd gathers around Mr. Graves and Mr. Arden. I notice Susie, the hostess from the club, walking about serving the crowd a plate of hors d'oeuvres. I say to Clare, "Let me go inside. I need to find the restroom and then we can go." My conscience will not allow me to tell Clare the true purpose of my visit inside.

I enter a side door and inside one of the staff immediately says, "Excuse me, sir. Guests should remain outside during the party."

I smile and reply, "Just looking for the restroom."

He replies, "Guests are asked to use the restroom in the pool house."

I counter with a quick lie, a skill easily honed and deployed with a mother as overbearing as mine, "I know, but someone has been in there for a while, and I cannot wait."

"Oh," says the young man. "It's down the hall. The third door on the right. Just be quick."

I walk down the hallway and admire the large oil paintings, each illuminated by a brass light over it. As I walk down the long hallway, I look down and admire the oversized Karastan rugs as I carefully peep into each room until I find what looks like Mr. Graves's home office.

I glance down the long hallway. No one has seen me, and I slip in and close the door.

Inside the library-like room sits a large mahogany desk. Behind it stands a large built-in bookshelf filled with glossy leather-bound decorative books with classical titles in gold lettering. In front of the desk sit two large brown leather chairs. On the side wall there is a small antique credenza containing large crystal decanters with varying amounts of brown liquid. Beside it is a slim pocket door.

I hurry over to the desk and glance at the few documents stacked on top, but nothing there is related to Cogniv-Pharma. I move around to the back of the desk and attempt to open the top drawer. It is locked. *Damn it.* I look around and with surprisingly little effort find the key on top of one of the shelved books.

I unlock and open the drawer, my heart pounds against my chest, my thoughts spiraling into erratic and irrational patterns. I take a deep breath and collect myself, but my hands still shake. I see a file labeled *RemMem*. I place it on the desk and open it. Inside, the names of each doctor listed on the subpoena stare back at me. Beside each name is a small ledger noting payment amounts and footnotes detailing debits from Mr. Graves's family foundation. There is no description for these payments, only the familiar scribble of Mr. Arden's signature beside each.

I continue to shift through the thick file, examining as many pages as I can, while the weight of its contents presses down on me.

In the desk drawers I see more files with tabs: *Clinical Trials* and *FDA Approval. These must contain the reasons behind the payments,* I think.

I open them. *Yes, this is what I thought.* I grab my iPhone and open the camera app, when suddenly I hear someone unlocking the pocket door. Panicked, I shut the desk drawer, leaving the documents on top and run to the other door. I grab the doorknob, but before I can leave, I hear a woman ask, "Excuse me, but what are you doing in here?"

I turn around. It is Susie. Slightly relieved, I respond, "I am just looking for the restroom."

She looks at me with her arms crossed and says in a short-tempered voice, "Well, it is not in here." She lowers her arms to take off her stained apron and gives me a false smile. "I am meeting Mr. Arden in here. I have something I need to tell him, so I suggest you get the hell out of here if you know what's good for you."

She seemingly does not recognize me as I hurry and leave the room to find Clare and go home.

During the drive home, I do not say a word about my clandestine efforts to discover the truth. The ride home is quiet until I grimace and say under my breath, "Shit." *I left the files on top of the desk.* Yet still, my mind races about what I found. *What does this mean? Why would Graves pay physicians out of his family foundation?*

Before turning home into our driveway, I notice a slight fog beginning to form when Clare asks, "John, what's on your mind? Usually after these parties you are full of comments."

"Nothing," I reply. My instincts still warn me not to tell Clare. I have no answers, plus, I had no business snooping in Mr. Graves's office. "Just ready to get home."

My mind will not stop. *Was this wrong, even if it was related to the subpoena?* My gut burns with questions and my heart aches with concerns about my moral and professional duty.

The dog days of summer come to an end and there is one more tournament of the season before I begin my senior year in high school, the state closed championship. This year's venue is Greenwood, South Carolina, a fifty-minute ride down Highway 28, meaning no hotel and long drives every day. Greenwood is a town very similar to Shoals and like Shoals is built around textile mills.

My mother stands beside me as I check into the tournament. One of the tournament hostesses recognizes me and says, "Good morning, John, and welcome. I have you all checked in. Here is your T-shirt. Are you interested in entering the talent show? It's the night of the tournament cookout."

I think about the piano, but before I can open my mouth my mother looks at me and says, "No, we don't have time for that."

I think to myself, *I have competed in tournaments against many of the same people since I was twelve and no one knows anything about me outside of tennis.*

The mundane ritual of tennis tournaments has remained unchanged. I linger, friendless, because each player is a potential opponent. My mother makes the drive each day seem longer with her incessant chatter about my talent or my opponent. Everything revolves around tennis and any attempt to steer the subject elsewhere is met with her stern, "Now, don't get yourself distracted." If we arrive early or if my match is delayed, I sit in the car with my mother, or we go to a nearby spot away from the tournament to sit in the air-conditioning.

Every tennis tournament is lonely. But for my mother, they seem to fulfill a need I do not understand. It gives her an energy, which sucks away at mine. Her pull exhausts me because it compels me to please my mother; and pleasing means winning. Losing means failure, which, for a son intent on being compliant, means opening a floodgate of unmanageable guilt, although I have done nothing wrong.

By this time of the season, I am tired and begin losing interest in tennis. I enjoy playing on the high school team, but tennis tournaments stress me out.

The state tournament starts just as it did the last few years. The draw shows I am a 9–16 seed. This is expected, but not good enough to meet my mother's expectations, just like my first two matches, which I win with little trouble.

My next match pairs me against a 5–8 seed and someone I have never played in a tournament. My opponent, a late starter to tennis, has risen fast through the rankings. Although he is the higher seed, my mix of heavy topspin forehands and slice backhands is too much for him. He struggles with my ability to change the pace of the rally and, when he approaches the net, my passing shots are unbelievable. I win the first set 6–4 after running down a deep approach shot and hitting a running forehand passing shot for a winner.

My confidence spills over when I see my opponent's father acting like my mother when I am losing to a lesser player. Somehow this inspires me on the next changeover, after having won the first game of the second set with a service ace blasted down the center line, to look over at his father and say, "There is a lot more of that coming."

I have complete control of the entire match. My groundstrokes are unmatched, and I am killing my serve. I feel light on my feet and my mind is clear. I win the second set 6–3. On the way home my mother laughs at the comment I made to the father. *Yeah, and if I had lost you would be yelling at me about being disrespectful and allowing his father to distract me.*

My next match, the quarterfinals, places me against the number two seed, a player I had beaten in high school matches and when we were much younger, but I had not played against him in a tournament in the last four years. Like me, his game centers on power.

During the drive, my mother discusses my upcoming opponent. "Now don't go out there and bang around groundstrokes. You have more talent and need to use it."

I only listen, although I want to reply, *No shit, Mom.*

She continues, "If you win you will be in the semifinals."

"I know, Mom."

I must have sounded short because my mother replies, "Don't get impatient with me. I need to you to go out there and play smart."

I do not respond.

"And don't get caught up with his friends who will be watching the match and get psyched out."

The more my mother talks the more nervous I grow until I see the Gatewood Club and Community sign. We arrive at the white guard shack surrounded by brilliant, flamboyant blooms of red crepe myrtles, a sensitive tree symbolizing good fortune. We pass the guard, and I roll down my window. In the tree-lined streets I hear the morning call of cardinals and wrens. This relaxes me until I realize my opponent is in the car behind us.

My mother sees him and his mother in the rearview mirror. I see my mother tighten her grip on the steering wheel. Feeling her tension, I take a deep breath. My mother accelerates her old, used BMW in hopes of creating some distance between us and my opponent in his mother's brand new, larger BMW. They accelerate with us.

My mother says to me, "She better get her fast ass off my bumper." She follows up her statement with another, "If your father was a doctor, I guess I would get a brand-new BMW every year, too."

We pull into a parking space by the courts, and they park beside us. My mother's frustration hangs at its threshold. This gives me an empty feeling and I want to escape the car. Thankfully, my mother does not delve into her repertoire of decisive actions. Instead, she huffs and sighs, until putting on a fake smile and getting out of the car, where my opponent's mother is waiting to talk.

"Good morning, Francis. How are the Greenburns today?"

I return a glance and a smile as I walk to the tournament desk to check in. I hear my mother's pithy reply, "Good morning."

It is obvious my mother does not want to engage in a conversation, but my opponent's mother continues, "We missed y'all last night at the cookout. There was a young lady who played the violin, and she was just lovely."

My mother replies, "We are not staying in town and needed to get home."

I check in with the tournament official, Ms. Garvin. A longtime tournament official for South Carolina tennis, she has known me since the beginning of my tennis days.

My heart sinks when Ms. Garvin says, "You will be playing on court number one." Court number one means everyone will be watching my match.

My mother walks over and asks, "What court are you on?"

"One," I reply with hesitation.

"Well, you know what to do."

The match begins with a furious intensity. We hit the ball hard, but consistently. During one point I marvel at my own power and how I have never hit the ball this hard in a match before. At the same time, my opponent is returning each shot with equal power and accuracy. This attracts many spectators, but I do not care. I enjoy the thrill of my play and continue to slug the ball with heavy topspin.

We are one hour into the match and still in the first set. Each game includes many deuces and the difference in who wins each game is razor thin. At 5–6, I win the deuce point by hitting a slice serve out wide to my opponent's forehand, which takes him almost to the next court. His return falls into the net, and I hear the crowd clapping with excitement. On the next point we rally back and forth until my opponent hits a low approach shot to my backhand and rushes the next. I hit the lowest percentage shot, a backhand topspin lob. It hits square on the baseline, and we are tied at 6–6.

The tiebreaker, like the first set, is grueling. Sweat flies off our heads with the stroke of each shot. When I bounce the ball in preparation to serve, I see droplets of sweat hitting the ground. The high sun beats down on us and the August humidity reminds everyone how summer's strong grasp still rules.

We continue our fight. Each point makes the winner holler in excitement and the loser groan in defeat. This attracts Ms. Garvin. She knows both of us, but more importantly appreciates how we both have a competitive temper.

At 6–5 in the tiebreaker, I hit a strong forward down the line and see my opponent is out of position. I rush the net and meet his weak return with an overhead smash winner that I hit with such force it bounces over the fence. We both simultaneously yell and during the changeover, Ms. Garvin says, "Boys, I need you to come over here."

Both of our shirts are dripping with sweat. We are both in need of a break. At the changeover we both drag our feet to Ms. Garvin. She looks at us and says, "Guys, you two are having an amazing match, but you both need to stay in control of yourself. Understood?"

"Yes, ma'am," we reply together, and I change into a fresh shirt and wring the sweat out of my old one like it had been thrown in the lake. As I put on the fresh shirt, I notice dried sweat on my eyeglasses. I wipe it off and carry the towel to the back of the court.

I serve first in the second set as our fierce battle continues shot for shot. At 30–30, sweat drips from my hair and covers my glasses, making it hard to see. Before serving, I grab my towel and begin to wipe off my glasses. I hear someone call my name. It is Ms. Garvin. She looks at me and says, "Play must be continuous."

I shake my head and serve the next point. Back and forth we pound the ball as we shuffle from side to side. After a long rally, my opponent's forehand sails long.

Again, sweat covers my glasses. As I go for my towel, I hear Ms. Garvin again say, "Play must be continuous. This is your first warning. The next time will be a point penalty."

I raise my hands and shrug as if to say, "What am I supposed to do?" I release my stress with my next serve and win the game with a service ace. Unfortunately, like tournaments prior, my competitive focus turns toward Ms. Garvin and my perception of her unfairness. During the changeover, I protest, "What am I supposed to do? I cannot see if I don't wipe off my glasses."

She responds, "Play must be continuous. You do not have time to wipe off your glasses after each point."

"Whatever," I reply with my brattiest voice.

I remain focused on Ms. Garvin and do not notice the physical changes in my opponent. The next three points are a continuation of our long, hard-fought rallies. I am up 40–love, when I see my opponent walk over to his chair.

Seeing this I whip my head at Ms. Garvin and begin my rant, "Now, wait a minute. How come he gets to?"

This is all I get out before I hear my mother: "John, hush!"

I freeze and stand at attention to my mother's irritable tone.

Ms. Garvin walks over and says, "Your opponent is taking a five-minute injury time-out."

I return her remark with a puzzled expression and look over at my opponent. He struggles with catching his breath. I see his mother hand him an inhaler. I never knew my opponent was asthmatic. He struggles another minute before taking a third huff from the inhaler. He stands by the fence with his mother until I hear Ms. Garvin yell, "Time."

As I prepare to serve, I think about how I have three consecutive game points. Rather than attempt another powerful serve, I hit a softer spin serve he returns. I intentionally do not attempt any winners. I want the point to last as long as possible. Seeing my opponent begin to struggle again, I surprise him with a drop shot. He rushes the net, and I meet his return with a lob. It sails over his head. He sprints and returns it. I hit another drop shot. He stands trying to catch his breath. When he finally does, he holds up his hand and shakes his head. "I cannot continue." My opponent goes to his mom for another dose from his inhaler and Mrs. Garvin declares me the winner. The match is over.

The next day I lose my semifinal match, and the following day I also lose the third-place playoff. The last time I finished in the top four I was ten years old. Satisfied, my mother does not even scold me for the two losses.

This was the last tournament and, on the way home, I thought about my ups and downs during the year. I desperately hoped they would balance themselves out and I would end the year with a high ranking.

We arrive home and before I can unload my gear upstairs in my room, my mother calls to me from the bottom of the stairs, "John, telephone call."

At the top of the stairs, I see my mother's sappy look, which matches her unusually sappy voice. As I descend, she continues to hold the cordless phone against her chest so the caller on the other end cannot hear her say, "It's the Citadel tennis coach."

On the other end of the phone a warm voice greets me, "John, this is Coach Boykin from down at the Citadel. I hope you are doing well and have had a good season."

Coach Boykin is nearing retirement age. He is an old-school coach in an affectionate and nostalgic way; he adheres to old-fashioned values and principles. His teams are a family and the atmosphere he creates is cohesive and supportive. Although he is fearless and demanding, he teaches his players how there is more to the game than just winning. He builds people, not just players. This is what attracts me the most to Coach Boykin and the Citadel: the opportunity to mature into a person.

"Yes, sir," I reply, "it was pretty good. Our school won its third state championship in a row, and I did well at the southern regional and state tournaments."

"Now, did I hear you just finished fourth at the state tournament?"

I try to remain calm and not show my nervousness. "Yes, sir, that's right."

Coach Boykin continues, "Yeah, some folks down here are still talking about that quarterfinal match."

Next, he changes the subject. "How's school going? Your grades, OK?"

I reply again, "Yes, sir. I should make the honor roll again this semester."

"That's great, John. Your parents must be really proud of you. A star on the court and in the classroom."

"I guess so, thanks, Coach."

"Well, listen, John, the reason I am calling is we would love for you to come down and take an official visit to the Citadel. We will treat you to a football game, give you some time to meet the players on the tennis team, and pair you with a cadet so you can tour the barracks, the campus, and sit in on a few classes."

I grin at the eureka moment. I had finally received the call I had been waiting for and all indication showed the Citadel was interested in me.

I reply, "Sure, that sounds great."

"Wonderful, how about you plan to be here in November? I will make you a reservation at the Hampton Inn by the Ashley River. Until then if you need anything give me a call. Sound OK?"

"Sure, Coach. I appreciate it and look forward to it."

"Great," replies Coach Boykin. "Anything else I can do for you?"

I hesitate, but cannot resist asking, "Coach, are you going to have a scholarship available for me?"

"Well now, John. Let's take this one step at a time. You come on down here in a few weeks and let's see how you fit in. We can discuss a scholarship once this year's rankings come out in January."

I lower my head and say, "OK, I appreciate it and will look forward to seeing you soon."

My mother hears me end the call and rushes into the kitchen, where I have been talking. She looks at me with an excited grin and asks, "So, what did he say?"

My disappointment sounds like sadness, "He wants me to come down for a visit in November."

My mother hugs me and says, "John, I am so proud of you."

I look at my mother and say, "But he said I had to wait before talking about a scholarship. He says he wants to see the new rankings first."

When we arrive home from Mr. Graves's party, I see Mary's bedroom light is on. I walk inside expecting to see her bottle-feeding her recent litter of foster kittens, but inside, she meets us in the hall with no kittens in sight. Her face ebbs and flows with emotion. "Dad, Poppy wants you to call him. He took Grammy to the hospital tonight. The doctor says she needs surgery."

As Mary finds peace in Clare's arms and surrenders her fears I rush to telephone my father, who answers in a sleepy voice. "John, your mom…she's OK, but, um…there is something I need to tell you…and it's serious."

Antsy, I reply, "What is it, Dad?"

I feel guilty about ignoring all the calls. Only Clare, knowing how stressed I have been at work, has reached out to him recently. I hear my father get out of bed and attempt to wake himself up. "Listen, your mom needs surgery. After y'all left, she started complaining of headaches. I finally convinced her to let me take her to the emergency department. She had a CT scan, and there was no bleeding from her fall, but the neurosurgeon, Dr. Winston, says she has a tumor on her pituitary gland."

"OK, but those are typically benign and do not have to be removed."

"Well, Dr. Winston says it's very large and touching the optic nerve. He believes it's affecting your mom's vision. You know she has been complaining about her eyesight for a while. Well, the doctor says if it does not come out, she could eventually go blind."

I imagine blindness added to Mom's current disposition and wince. It will make it impossible for my father to care for her. He will never survive. None of us will survive.

My voice fills with hesitation as I ask, "So, Dad, what's the plan?"

"Dr. Winston has scheduled her for surgery, but first she needs to get clearance from her family physician and go for pre-op testing at the hospital."

"OK, but, Dad, why did you not call me sooner tonight about this?"

"Well, son," my father pauses for a moment, "I knew you were at your work party and didn't want to bother you and Clare on your evening out."

I attempt to process the potential enormity of this situation. Anesthesia will accelerate and worsen my mother's memory loss. My mind races as I blurt out, "We can't let her just go blind. That would be horrible. What about—"

My father interrupts, "John, can you come to South Carolina for your mom's surgery?"

Inside my mind, I hear my mother's voice reminding me, *You will feel guilty the rest of your life if something happens to me. You may never see me again. Do you want my last thought of you to be, why was John not here?*

"Of course I will be there."

CHAPTER SIXTEEN

My mother's surgery is quickly scheduled. Weighted with unspoken worries, I load the car as the children surround me with anxious faces. I reassure everyone that my mother's particular surgery is performed often and that her doctor is very competent. I hug Clare and make a last rhetorical plea, "Don't you think it would be better if you went? You're a nurse, and I think Mom would do better if you were there."

Clare gives me a smile. "She's your mother. It's more important you're there."

I know she is right, so I hug her and get in the car as she says, "It'll be fine. You know what to do."

The route to my parents' house, long and weary, covers a monotonous stretch of interstate. I listen to music and podcasts, hoping to relieve the tension in my mind, a futile attempt to slow the rising tide of worry that fills me. Other than driving, I can only think about how I will survive the next few days, especially when my mother comes home to recover. She will be frail and unable to do much, and she'll have little stamina.

Their house creates a challenge, too. It does not have a full bathroom downstairs, and all the bedrooms are upstairs. My mother says, refusing to acknowledge the burden, "Oh, I will just sleep on the couch." Although the couch has stood as her sanctuary through the years, a refuge from her tirades of grief, it will not suffice for the trials to come. She will need more comfort, more support, than its worn cushions can offer, as the weight of her recovery settles in.

I think to myself, *How am I going to deal with this and all the stuff going on at work? I am so close to figuring out everything behind this subpoena.*

I have no answers. I must wait until I learn more.

My father and I sit in the surgery waiting room. I watch the scrolling color-coded board update families about their loved ones' surgeries. My mother is still in pre-op holding. A lady with a hospital badge pushing a computer on a cart approaches my father. She says, "Hi, are you Mr. Greenburn?"

My father gives her a defensive look and replies, "Yeah." My skin curls, hoping my father will be patient and courteous.

Unphased by my father's rigid posture, she continues, "Hi. I just need to get some financial information about your wife. Let's see. We have her Medicare information and the information for her supplemental policy. So, the only thing we need is her social security number."

Oh boy, I think to myself, *here we go. My father has watched too much political news to trust anyone with a social security number, especially a hospital.*

"What the hell do you need that for?"

"Please refrain from cursing at me, Mr. Greenburn. It's just that I need it to finish registering her financial information into our system so we can bill Medicare."

My father narrows his eyes. His thick, dark steel eyebrows stretch downward. "I don't think so. You don't need that information. You already have everything you need."

"OK, Mr. Greenburn. I understand."

Obviously, my father is not the first conspiracy theorist she has dealt with. It seems as if today the world is filled with them. Pulling her cart away, she turns and says, "Thank you, Mr. Greenburn. I hope everything goes well with your wife."

I sense my father has had enough and will not answer, so I turn and give a polite thank you.

The surgeon removes the tumor, and my mother stays in the hospital to recover. On the first day I study her profile while she rests in the bed. My mother is remarkably pretty for seventy-nine. I follow the curve of her nose and see the resemblance of my youngest daughter, Vivian. Before I leave for the night, I stop by the hospital chapel and give thanks. There were no side effects of the memory drug. It did not cause any complications. I still wonder if I need to ask. *I'm sure it is in her medical record. Dr. Knuckles is employed by the hospital, so they must use the same medical record.* This thought satisfies me for the moment.

I return to my parents' house. The male two-spotted tree crickets welcome me with their gentle chirping. The warm and humid night weather inspires their fast high pitch, which is made louder as they chew holes into the leaves they then place their wings up against while singing. At the same time, I hear the unmistakable kay-tee-did-kay-tee-did notes of the male katydids singing their love songs into the euphoria of the sultry summer night.

I stand in the dark and listen. The sounds embrace me. For the first time in years, I stand at the house I grew up in and feel love surround me. It transcends reality.

The next afternoon, my mother sits up in the bed and fixes her steel gray hair. When I enter her room, I resent the ache in my heart that makes it difficult for me to speak. My mother and I have not had an actual conversation in years. Before her dementia, her anger at my living so far away caused me to keep our conversations on the surface. She and I know why I moved away years ago, but we never discuss it.

"How are you feeling, Mom?"

She looks up, and I see an orange stain on the bandage above her lip. "I am doing good, so long as your dad keeps getting me orange sherbet."

I look over at my father. He says, "That is about all she feels like eating for now."

My mother raises her head and asks my father, "Did you bring me my bottle of wine?"

In his best attempt to be reasonable, my father raises his eyebrows and replies, "Francis, you are in the hospital. You can't have wine here."

"Who says?" she retorts, curling her face in rebuttal. "If you bring me a bottle, I don't see why they would not let me have just a little bit."

I think to myself, *Less than two days, and she is already starting to have withdrawal. This will get old very quickly.*

The nurse comes in and checks my mother's vital signs. Before she leaves, the nurse asks, "Is there anything I can get you, Mrs. Greenburn?"

My mother grins like a fox in a henhouse and says, "No, unless you can get me a little glass of wine."

The nurse giggles and says, "I'm sorry. I can get you just about anything but that."

My father turns on the hospital television. The French Open is playing. I clench my teeth and cringe. As a teenager, I hated watching tennis on television. I never fully understood why I disliked watching it other than I was incapable of living tennis twenty-four hours a day like the rest of my family.

I know that comments about my tennis-playing days are coming next, so I change the subject by introducing dinner. "Dad, are you planning to stay here all night?"

"Yes," he replies. His duty to my mother has always been clear. At eighty, he stands by her side even if it means sleeping in a vinyl recliner in the hospital room.

Expecting his answer, I ask, "But what about dinner?"

"I'll be OK here. I can find something down in the cafeteria."

I roll my eyes and say, "Dad, you've been up here all day sitting. Why don't you go home for a little bit? Mom can rest, and you can take a shower. While you are showering, I will fix us some dinner."

"Well, OK. I guess. What time is it now?"

"It's 3:30," I reply. "Why don't you stay up here a little longer until Mom goes back to sleep? I will go by the grocery store and get stuff to make dinner."

My father gives a forced consent and says, "Now, don't go to too much trouble, and don't dirty up the kitchen. Your mom will have a fit."

I take a last look at my mother, who is eating another orange sherbet, and say, "I am going now. I hope you have a good night, and I will send Dad back once I feed him."

"OK, I'll be fine. The nurses are taking good care of me. Just don't forget the wine next time."

I examine my mother's hand with its long, slim fingers. She has never gotten a manicure, but her nails look perfect. My mind tells me to hold her hand before I leave. Instead, I say, "You are looking good, Mom. If you look this good tomorrow, I may sneak in that glass of wine for you."

She perks up and says, "Don't you worry about that. I will be ready."

CHAPTER SEVENTEEN

At the grocery store, I pick out a thick salmon fillet at the seafood counter. Salmon has always been one of my father's favorite meals, unless it is salmon from a can cooked into salmon cakes. Growing up, salmon cakes made from canned salmon sitting on the dinner table was a definite signal that my mother was angry at my father. As I grew older, I learned how during the Great Depression the federal government subsidized canned salmon. During this time mill hands at Shoals Mill could buy a can of salmon for a nickel. I wonder if this mill hill history added to my family's bitterness.

I grab a package of butter, eggs, and milk and hope everything else I need is at the house.

Next, I stop at Concord Market, the jewel of every trip home. Here, I take my time selecting beautiful Granger City, Tennessee, tomatoes. Each is a fire-engine red softball with succulent insides. I grab several with plans for BLTs later in the in the week. I grab a pound of butter beans and Silver Queen corn, and ask how often a new shipment arrives, knowing my family's jealousy will cause them to retaliate in anger if I do not bring some home. Finally, I place a basket of McBee peaches on the counter and grab a carton of Clemson vanilla ice cream from the portable freezer section of the outdoor market.

Before I get out of the car at my parents' house, I hesitate and think how this may be the first time I have ever been in the house alone. Throughout my entire life, even as an adult, my mother's constant supervision ensured she or my father was always at the house when I was there. Thinking this makes me chuckle as I get out of the car and walk into the house.

Like the entire house, my mother's kitchen is pristine. Her five-year-old oven looks like it has never been cooked in. The stovetop with no scratches looks the same. The new countertops are covered with large cutting boards so that nothing touches them. The high-end dishwasher my parents bought two years ago still looks pristine, because they still handwash everything.

In the kitchen, everything is organized as it has been for the last thirty years. This allows me to find the things I need. I quickly peel the peaches to prepare them for the cobbler. I question the age of the flour, sugar, and baking powder but have no choice other than to use them or return to the store. The beans simmer on the stove in the one chicken bouillon cube I found in the pantry.

Inside the refrigerator, there is plenty of room for the salmon. Only a few slices of deli ham and cheese sit on the shelves. The bottom drawer holds a head of iceberg lettuce, and the door compartments contain a variety of expired dressings and condiments, which I toss into the garage trash can. Finally, I open the freezer. Again, no surprises, as I count three cartons of ice cream plus the one I purchased.

While waiting for my father, I pour a hefty glass of wine and stroll around the backyard. Much of my parents' yard is wooded, and the trees provide welcoming shade for me and homes for various birds. I hear a pair of pileated woodpeckers call each other to a tree, where they scamper together in search of bugs. After one go-around of the tree, they fly off, giving their distinct Woody Woodpecker trill.

A brilliant bluebird lands on the birdhouse in the front yard and makes his way inside. I make a mental note to remind my father.

Next, I go down to the creek. Recent rains have washed away much of the bank. Looking for life, such as a possible salamander, I spy something unusual yet familiar. Using my index finger, I dig around the edges of my find and realize it is a plastic army figure, likely from my preteen days, when my friends and I set up World War II battles on the banks of the small creek. After many battles, all but a few of the plastic figures are washed down the creek toward the pond.

At the pond, I observe two young boys fishing. They are undoubtedly brothers, as I listen to them banter about who will catch the most and the biggest fish. I also see my father crossing the bridge into the neighborhood and hurry back inside to finish dinner.

When my father enters the side door by the garage, I hear him say, "John, what smells so good?"

"Dinner," I proudly announce.

My dad enters the kitchen. "Wow, look at all of this."

"That's not all, Dad, I got a nice piece of salmon I am about to put in the oven."

My father's eyes grow big as he asks, "You didn't forget the cornbread, did you?"

I laugh heartily, "Dad, cornbread mix was about all you had between the pantry and the refrigerator. I counted six boxes."

He replies, "I got ice cream, too."

"I know, Dad. I saw all the cartons in the freezer."

"Well, you know I like ice cream."

During dinner, my father and I talk unlike we ever have before. We do not discuss my mother's surgery, and we do not carefully avoid topics that always lead to bruised feelings. Instead, my father displays a unique charm, sharing stories about growing up in Shoals Mill.

My favorite story is the one about my uncle Bull, who did not like going to high school.

My father starts, "Each day my daddy pulled up to the school in his Falcon wagon to drop us off. In those days, the principal stood in the driveway, waved at the parents, and greeted the students as they arrived.

"Well, each Monday Frog Reames, who was the principal, waved to Daddy and said hello to Bull and me. Then Bull proceeded to walk into the front door and straight out the back door of the school. He'd go fishing or go down to the pool hall and play the pinball machines.

"He did this for fourteen straight Mondays until one Monday my daddy got locked out of the house. When that happened, he called the school and asked to speak to Bull, because Bull had the extra key to the house. Daddy sure was surprised when Frog told him, 'Mr. Greenburn, this is the fourteenth Monday your boy has missed school.'"

I ask my dad, "What happened to Bull?"

He snickers and simply replies, "Well, he did not ever skip school again."

I am struck by the relaxed look on my father's face as he remembers each story. I am struck even more by the joy each story brings out.

As we talk my father reminds me, "Growing up on the mill hill meant when everyone else started running, you ran, too.

"I remember this one time a group of us were walking home from a ball game and someone started running. Now, in the mill village, when someone started running it usually meant someone pulled a fire alarm or threw a rock at a house.

"We all started running and I heard a police siren behind us, so I jumped into the back seat of an unlocked car. The next thing you know the guy who owned the car got in to leave for the third shift. I knew the man and figured it was not far, so I just stayed in the car until he got to the mill. Once he was inside, I got out and walked home."

As the night continues, my father describes pranks he and his friends pulled on old ladies who did not return baseballs that landed in their yards. He talks about his uncle Claude, sneaking him to chicken fights. He replays his days on the gridiron at Boys High School and winning the football state championship. It is nice to see him so at ease.

Then my father's light voice changes. His eyes soften with an inner glow. "John, have I ever told you how my daddy was invited to be an assistant women's basketball coach at Clemson?"

I reply, "Really? I did not know that."

"Yes, he was. Annie Tribble was the coach back then. She was from town and knew my daddy especially well because he coached several high-school-aged women's recreation league teams, including your mother's team.

"I was visiting Daddy when she came over to his house and sat down in the den. She said, 'Grinny, I can work around whatever your schedule needs to be. You don't have to give any speeches and you don't have to travel to out-of-town games. But I need you to find me talented players. You know just about every young lady who plays basketball in these parts, and I need you to bring them to Clemson.'

"My daddy stood up and as he walked over to the window said, 'Coach Tribble, I remember you playing here during college. You were a heck of a player.' He stopped at the window and pushed back the curtains and continued, 'Coach, look down that street all the way down to Shoals Mill. See all those families living in those houses? Each one of those families is expecting me to coach their kids.'

"Coach Tribble smiled and said, 'Grinny, that's what makes you such a great coach and a treasure to this community.' She paused and said, 'I appreciate you letting me come by.'"

My father, with his voice full of pride, says, "John, that was the type of person your grandfather was. Always looking out for other people he knew were counting on him, and never for himself or fame."

When my father finishes with his stories, I share stories about my job and my visits to Capitol Hill in Washington, D.C. He listens to every detail. His eyes grow large when I tell him about being in individual meetings with senators. "You actually sat in a meeting with a senator who once ran for president? What was that like?"

He beams with pride when I tell him about defending cases in front of the Department of Justice. "You mean the federal government? The same people who sometimes investigate the president?"

He displays charm as he asks questions about my role as an attorney. At one point he says, "Son, I had no idea how important your job is. You have worked very hard and achieved lots."

When we finish our ice cream and peach cobbler, my father turns deep and serious. I see he is preparing for something, but it is not another story. He thinks long and hard about something. For a moment we sit in quiet stillness until he begins, "Son, I know your mom was hard on you a lot when you were younger. She just wanted you to have things easier than the way she had them. Growing up on the mill neither one of us had much."

Then he looks me in the eye, which causes him to get choked up with emotion. As his voice cracks and a tear rolls down his cheek he says, "Your mom and I are really proud of you. You have accomplished more than we ever imagined and most importantly you are a really good father and husband. You are a family man, first."

I know it took courage for my cautious and reserved father to say what he did, which gave his simple statement a power beyond the Holy Scriptures. But I want to know more and say, "But, Dad, what about the mill?"

Before my father replies, I watch him reach deep, down to the bone. "Son, we had fun growing up on the mill and we were all like one large family looking out for each other. But at the same time, it was a hard life. We were poor and did not have much. People outside of the mill looked at us differently. They disparaged us. They called us 'white trash' or 'lintheads.' If you came from the mill hill, others did not give you the same opportunities, just look at your mom."

"Mom? What do you mean?"

"Son, your mom was one hell of a mathematician. She could make my paycheck go farther than I ever imagined. I used to think she could take a couple of one-dollar bills and turn them into a five."

I give a light chuckle and say, "Yeah, I remember all those times she sat at the desk reconciling old checks to her ledger. It had to be down to the penny before she would quit."

My father smiles and replies, "That's right, just like she expected you to work on the tennis court and do you know why?"

"Not really."

"It's because she never had the opportunities like the ones that have presented themselves to you."

"What do you mean, Dad?"

"Look at all the doors tennis has opened for you. Think about the number of people you have met. Think about how tennis taught you to survive on your own and succeed." My father attempts to relax his tense muscles and then continues, "Your mother was a woman in the 1960s and 1970s. Do you think businesses looked at women from the mill hill and offered them jobs? Hell no."

I give my father a puzzled looked and reply, "But Mom was a schoolteacher."

"Yes," my father gets up from his chair and begins pacing the kitchen floor. "And that was her only opportunity. Plus, she hated teaching school. Your mother wanted to be an accountant and could have run circles around any man at any business in town, but those jobs were held for other people, and for certain women who did not come from the mill hill." He pauses for a moment and looks at me with desperation. "That's why your mother pushed you so hard. She never wanted you to suffer the disappointment she lived with, always feeling like she was not good enough, and how the mill took so much from her."

Later in the night I'm preparing for bed when my iPhone buzzes. I look down expecting to see that it's Clare calling to say good night. Instead, it flashes Cogniv-Pharma. *I'll be damned if I am going to end my night dealing with Mr. Graves. What a bastard!* I throw my iPhone down on the bed and go the bathroom and brush my teeth.

I come back and turn off the lights. I lie in bed. The moon, which rose with the setting of the sun, calls for my presence and asks for reflection. I listen to the ancient spiritual chorus of the cicadas finish their cacophony of prophecies about being resurrected upon the top of a tree. I enjoy sitting in this transcendent realm of my own personal transformation. I cherish the evening and take in how my father embraced my spiritual core.

The iPhone clatters against the bedside table. Without looking I grab it. Holding it up in the dark I see again, Cogniv-Pharma. I do not understand why the company name appears. I only assume it is Mr. Graves. Again, I do not answer. I want to enjoy the moment.

I quickly fall asleep as the shadowy new moon crosses the sky, keeping its illuminated face away from earth. Vivid dreams enter my mind. Emotions rise throughout my body as I sit by two streams flowing in different directions. One flows in the direction of a green sea filled with money. Around it, people fight for a place on the shore to fill their canvas bags. I watch the madness as people fill their bags too heavy to move. Others do not realize their bag has a hole and is empty by the time they leave the shore. I back away and see the formless void.

The other stream is pure, crystal clear. Its babble creates a serenade as its misty spray hits my face and gives me energy. I look in the stream and see life creating one form after another. People come to the stream from faraway places. Most of them are artists seeking solace from the confinement of reality. I listen to their music as it fills the air with sweetness. I watch them paint and sketch as their canvases create life. Others recite poetry as words flow from their mouths like the beautiful song of a sparrow on a treetop celebrating the day.

This river does not flow into the sea. Instead, a mighty dam stops the stream from flowing into an empty crater of dry cracked land, an extinct sea once full of life. As the stream nears the top of the dam its waters brighten with hope. However, the dam is made of empathy and grows taller and wider each time I absorb the feelings and priorities of others.

I walk into the stream and understand how its waters are my story. With each step I feel lighter, like a burden has been lifted from my shoulders. The water begins to swell and rush, forming into small rapids. It pushes me toward the dam. When I arrive against the dam, I see a crack and it begins to shake uncontrollably, ready to burst open.

Suddenly, I awaken, damp with sweat and full of emotional intensity. I can still hear the dam shake when I realize it is my phone. Again, Cogniv-Pharma. I do not know the time, but I answer. "Hello, this is John Greenburn."

"John, I apologize for calling at such a late hour, but I had to speak with you."

The reality of my world begins to return. Hesitant, I reply, "Mrs. Verity?"

Mrs. Verity is a board member of Cogniv-Pharma. She is the only female and the only board member who does not rubber stamp each of Mr. Graves's and Mr. Arden's requests. Like me, she has continued to question RemMem, and the speaker program used to promote it.

Mrs. Verity has always been a kindred spirit and good friend. Prior to retiring, she was the chief pharmacist at a major academic medical school. She holds numerous patents, has published over a hundred peer-reviewed articles, and recently published a literary novel.

"Yes, John, this is Maria Verity." I hear the desperation in her voice. "I should not be calling you, but I needed to tell you what happened." I hear her take a deep breath and swallow her emotions, "I have been dismissed from the board."

I rise out of the bed and sit on its side. "What? Dismissed from the board? How can they do that? What happened?"

"John," she replies with the voice of a mother soothing a child, "it's all right. My voice never mattered, and it will never matter."

"Never mattered?" I interject. "It was the only voice of reason that rose above the bullshit."

My rant short, she continues, "John, it's simple. This is all about RemMem. Mr. Arden did not tell me why, but I suspect people are beginning to ask questions and they do not need me speaking out at future board meetings."

I only say, "I understand."

"John, listen to me, as your friend. You know who you are dealing with. Do not allow this to consume you. You have too much emotional intelligence to waste on this matter. Plus, regardless of what happens, this situation with the Department of Justice will never define you professionally. Like I have told you before, you have too much substance. Follow your instinct and rise above this mess."

When she finishes, I take a moment to collect my thoughts. Of course, she can't know the risks I've taken to investigate what's been going on. I say, "Mrs. Verity, I appreciate you letting me know. You have always been kind to me, and I appreciate your willingness to speak up. I will miss you."

"Thank you, John. I will miss you, and please do not tell anyone I called you. At the next board meeting you must act like you do not know."

In September, after the summer of tennis tournaments, Hurricane Hugo makes landfall near McClellanville, SC. Days prior, my mother and father pace the floor, wondering if my older brother, a senior cadet at the Citadel a few miles south of McClellanville in Charleston, SC, will be evacuated. He arrives home with his roommate the day before landfall.

Hugo's landfall is 250 miles away, but its morning wind awakens me with eerie sounds as the tall white oaks on our wooded lot sway like a gospel choir.

My family and I watch the news in awe. "A Category Five storm. The costliest hurricane on record. The strongest hurricane since Hurricane Camille, 1969." Hugo breaks every record, and we watch videos from helicopters flying over the coast. Demolished homes, boats on top of houses, other boats piled up like children's toys, and the unforgettable pictures of the dangling Ben Sawyer Bridge, a swing bridge that connects the town of Mount Pleasant with Sullivan's Island.

The day after Hurricane Hugo makes landfall, my father's mother, Vivian, suffers a life-ending stroke. We wait for the ambulance, and I hear her pray. Listening to her, I know her faith is giving her comfort and helping her to overcome her pain.

A few weeks later, I'm watching the World Series when Candlestick Park begins to shake. Once it stops, players frantically look for their families, many crying, and hurry them out of the stadium. The baseball game is postponed. The news begins, showing the impacts of the magnitude 6.9 earthquake.

As I watch, I suddenly hear my parents yell, "John, we have to check on your grandfather." I think nothing of it until about an hour later, when there is a knock on the door. Our neighbor greets me and says, "John, your parents asked that I come over and share that your grandfather had a massive heart attack watching the YMCA softball game. The umpire performed CPR, and the ambulance got him to the hospital, but that's all I know."

Weeks later, he dies, never leaving the hospital.

November arrives and I make my college visit to the Citadel, at the invitation of Coach Boykin. From Columbia, South Carolina, and into Charleston, nothing but destruction. Interstate medians are full of fallen pine trees. Billboards on I-26 are bowed like singers leaving the stage. Destruction and loss are everywhere, both on the side of the interstate and in my heart.

CHAPTER EIGHTEEN

The next day, I arrive at my mother's room to a symphony of alarms. Doctors and nurses rush in and begin manipulating the machines and my mother at the same time. They ask my father and I to leave. The door slams with a bang. As I pace in the hallway, I hear muffled commands and sounds of chaos coming through the room window. My brain is unable to unscramble what is happening.

Suddenly, a team of nurses exit and rush my mother down the hall. A doctor rushes to my father and asks him to sign a consent for emergency surgery. My father scribbles his name as the doctor says, "Something has caused her surgical site to fail."

I am dumbstruck as I watch my father weep. I have never seen him cry before. My mind tells me it is his way of preparing for the inevitable, as darkness takes control of my mother's body. We sit in the waiting area in silence. I attempt to find words, but I am paralyzed by the many memories holding me silent. I am paralyzed more wondering if RemMem had anything to do with this.

After several hours, a nurse escorts us to the neuro ICU, where she explains that a leak from my mother's original surgical site opened, causing cerebral spinal fluid to flow into her cranium and place pressure on her brain.

The surgeon who repaired the leak enters. His confidence fills every void in the room. He explains that he repaired the leak and assures us it will hold.

I am desperate to ask the surgeon if he is familiar with RemMem and if my mother's condition and the surgical complications may be related to the drug. But before I can speak the surgeon says, "All we can do now is wait and see how soon the air and fluid is reabsorbed. But I expect her to make a full recovery."

I see the glow of optimism on my father's face and hold my tongue. As much as I want to ask about RemMem, I do not want to erode the positive news he has received. I think to myself, *I will call Dr. Pong later.*

My father walks over to the surgeon and gives him a strong handshake. "Now, Dr. Jorge, how long do you expect for that to take?"

Dr. Jorge leans back and glances out the window, "Oh, I'd say about two to three days. Like I said, once it is reabsorbed, she will be fully recovered."

A smile returns to my father's face, and he asks, "At that point we can go home, right?"

Dr. Jorge returns the smile and says, "I do not see why not."

During the entire conversation my gaze never leaves my mother. I watch her limp body and cannot fathom how she will find the strength to make a full recovery, let alone return home in two to three days. My mother, nearly eighty, has had a hole in her skull repaired. This haunting whisper of uncertainty fills my mind, affirming this notion's incomprehensibility. Even more, Dr. Jorge's unwavering confidence annoys me, and I worry his reassurances will fill my father with false hope.

Before the surgeon leaves, he hands us photos from my mother's surgery, taken through the endoscope. I look at them and think, *Why is he giving these to us? They are meaningless.*

My father thanks the surgeon as he leaves. As the door closes, my father looks at me and says, "Did you hear that? He expects your mother to have a full recovery."

Doctors who make predictions with certainty can be dangerous. I reply, "I guess. Let's take this one day at a time. I mean, he sure seems optimistic."

Day after day, I sit by my mother's bed with my father, looking down at her fragile form. She has been unresponsive for the last two days, ever since coming out of surgery. At least now, her eyes are open, but she does not focus on anything. Instead, she gives only a blank, mindless stare. Her dull, emotionless look suggests to me a minimally conscious state. At times, she waves her arms in front of her, as if she sees something that is not there.

From her room's window I can see the escarpment, where the majesty of the Blue Ridge meets the rolling foothills. Each day, rain, wind, and rivers subtly alter the mountains, reshaping them in the slightest of ways.

I look at my mother. I long to feel her energy, but I feel nothing. There are no changes to her condition. She does not look like a broken woman. Her face looks full, as if she could open her eyes at any moment, ready to walk out. However, each day, she grows frailer. Like the mountains I see from her room, nature's cycle of life is eroding her body and taking her away.

During my teen years when my mother's grief was at its worst, she would proclaim, "I think I will just lie down and die." I watch my mother's unconscious body in the hospital bed and wonder each day, *Is that what she is doing?*

My father asks, "John, do you think she is getting better?"

I reply, "It's hard to tell, Dad." I know she is dying, but I cannot tell him. I just say, "It is too early."

Did the RemMem do this to her?

At times, it appears my mother struggles to form words. Her mouth moves, but no sound escapes, and worse, her face remains void of expression. My father and I attempt to decipher her silent efforts, but she cannot help us understand.

Each day, the hospitalist physician arrives and examines my mother with her greatest thought and care. She suggests, "If there is no change in the next day or so, we may need to consider a palliative care consult."

Her words bring tears to my eyes as I watch my father stand at my mother's bed and hold her hand. Each hour he leans close and whispers, "I love you to the moon and back," a mantra of devotion and desperation.

Each day my brother calls my father. They talk for only a few minutes until he asks, "How's Mom doing?" Then he always ends the call with, "Let me know if anything changes."

My father uses the speaker on his phone for every call. Their conversations echo throughout the room. I overhear everything and think to myself, *Nothing is going to change until the end.*

When my father ends one call, I see my mother turn her head slowly and fix her gaze at him. Their eyes meet and I witness the raw emotions etched in my mother's face—remorse and terror mingled together. Her lips move, but no sound emerges, yet I am certain she is saying, "I am sorry."

Deep within me I feel the resonance of her words; her voice reaches a place where I hear it one last time, pure and clear, yet punctuated by something greater I cannot understand.

We wait by the bedside, each day chipping away a piece of my heart. A hole of nothingness grows in the middle of my body, an emptiness that deepens with the silence surrounding us, a silence more desolate than the void itself.

On the fourth day, I sit in the room with my father, the quiet between us thick with unspoken sorrow. A new nurse enters, interrupting our silent vigil. She introduces herself with a smile of concern before turning to my mother to assess her.

She evaluates her and begins administering her daily medicine into the IV machine. Her hands hold many vials of medicine. She attempts to look at my mother's hospital wristband, but fumbles around, almost dropping a syringe full of fluid. She gathers herself, looks at me, and politely asks, "Sir, can you read to me the full name and birthdate on your mom's armband? I need to verify it before giving this to her."

I think each medication dosage is either futile or merely delaying my mother's inevitable end. My only concern is finding the best time to encourage my father to move my mother to the town's hospice house, where her suffering might finally come to rest.

Regardless of my thoughts, I hold my mother's hand to look at her wrist. I can feel her bones. I have never seen her look so helpless. I read, "Francis R. Greenburn, August 29, 1943."

The nurse says, "Thank you," and begins administering the medications.

I do not release my mother's frail hand, unwilling to let go. I look at the wristband once more and read it to myself. A spark ignites within me. I look at my father, who deliberately turns away and looks out the window. I read it one more time, the words etched in my mind, each letter a thread pulling me deeper into a growing awareness.

The nurse looks at me and asks, "Is there anything you need?"

"No," I reply, hoping she does not sense my excitement.

When I hear the door latch click, I look over to my father and say, "Dad, this is wrong. Mom's middle initial is *C*. Her maiden name is Craft. Why is there an *R*?"

Tension fades from my father's face, giving way to a quiet empathy. The foundational element of a functional family enters his soul as I witness him freeing himself from the past, as though a long-possessing specter is exorcised from his soul, leaving behind a semblance of peace. "Son, her maiden name is Rex. Not Craft. Hazel is not your mother's *real* mother." My father's eyes look toward heaven as he searches for the right words. "Son, let's go somewhere and talk."

We walk outside to the healing garden, where majestic oaks surround the spiritual walking path and provide us with a serene veil of shade. This natural cathedral engages our senses with smells of lavender and tea olive, and the flow of water into the reflection pond sings to our ears. We find a bench and sit.

Seeing the strain in my father's eyes, I am concerned this is too emotional for him and say, "Dad, we don't have to do this now. It can wait."

My father, so ready to close the door on my mother's embattled past whenever I brought it up, begins in a distant and worn voice, as though the weight of old sorrows has finally found its way to his lips. "No, son," he replies, "your mother's past is complex, and I need to tell you the truth. The truth is your mother's real name is Francis Rex. Her mother is not Hazel. Her real parents were Ruth and Marlowe Rex."

I interrupt my father and ask, "You mean the guy who owned old Shoals Mill?"

"Yes," replies my father, "But back then his father James ran it while Marlowe courted Ruth as his mistress. Ruth did not believe her coworker's warnings, 'Rich boys don't marry lintheads,' until the day she discovered she was carrying Marlowe's baby."

I ask, "So, my real grandmother's name was Ruth?"

My father nods. Teary eyed, he heaves a weighty sigh and continues, "Your mother never told me much more, other than when her mother's pregnancy was discovered, Ruth and her grandfather, Robert Henry Keyt, were chased out of town by Mr. Rex's henchman—a guy everyone called Judge. Robert Henry returned to his hometown in the Piedmont only to find it at the bottom of a lake. He was never seen again.

"Ruth fled to a maternity house in Charlotte, North Carolina, run by a group called Christian Sisters. They helped her give birth to your mother, who was placed in the orphanage. A few months later, Ruth returned to Shoals Mill confronted Marlowe. He refused to acknowledge their relationships and the baby. When she learned he had married and had merely used her for pleasure, she ended her life by jumping off the trestle bridge that crosses the Rocky River. Her body was never found, but some say you can hear the cries of a baby if you stand on the bridge at night."

Amazed, I respond, "But how did mom figure all of this out?"

"Son," my father says, his voice low, drawn from some deep well of memory, "that's where Hazel comes in. Your mother was never adopted and ran from that orphanage when she was thirteen. The only information she had about her family was her mother's name, Ruth, and the address 14 C Street, Shoals Mill."

My father pauses, eyes clouded over, with a distant gaze. "When your mother arrived at 14 C Street Hazel and her family were living in that house."

I begin pulling at the loose threads of the story, the fragments of a past that feels like it's just beyond my reach. "So, that's when Mom started living with Hazel?"

He nods, slowly. "Yeah. She had nowhere else to go, no kin. Hazel took her in, gave her a place. Hazel became her mother. That's how it was back then—the mill families, they didn't let their own go without. They took care of each other, always. Even when the world around 'em didn't."

The words hang in the air like something old, something worn down by time but still there, still heavy. I stare out into the hospital garden, trying to catch the shape of my mother's life, the way it shifts and slips, like trying to hold water in cupped hands. Every piece of her story seems to explain something, but I know there's more, much more, buried in the quiet, hidden beneath all the years she spent trying to forget.

"Dad," I say, my voice low, uncertain. "Did Mom ever tell you anything else? There's got to be more about her, about Robert Henry... And who was her real grandmother?"

My father's eyes meet mine, that same sadness that clings to him now, always just beneath the surface. "That's all she ever said," he replies, his voice a dry rasp, like the rustle of dead leaves on the ground. "I tried. I asked her, I asked the old folks at the mill. But nobody wanted to talk. It's like they all just...decided it was best forgotten."

Then, like some spirit moved him, my father does what I never expected. He reached out, his hands trembling, and places them firm on my shoulders. "But you... You need to find out. The family needs to know. You need to do that for all of us."

"Know what, Dad?" I ask, the words barely forming.

"The rest of it. Your mother's whole story. Look what not knowing has done to us."

And in that moment, I feel something pass between us, something heavy and ancient, like the weight of stones carried through generations. It settles on my shoulders, sinking deep into my bones. But strange as it is, I also feel my mother's fire, burning inside me, giving me strength I did not know I had.

Telling my mother's story gives my father peace. Like so many who grew up as part of Shoals Mill, my mother lived to forget her past. Bound by the harsh realities of her worldly existence, my mother held little patience for the reality of this twittering world. *Now, I know. Now, I understand. I will eventually discover the rest.*

My father reminds me, "Son, the mill took everything from your mother. Her family, her youth, her life."

"Why did Mom never talk about this?"

"John, I guess your mom was determined to live her life close to the bone. However, one thing was certain. She always wanted you to have a better life than her and she would do anything to ensure that."

CHAPTER NINETEEN

My mother always opened my mail. No matter what the contents were, or if she already knew what the envelope contained, there was no privacy. So, I am not surprised to walk into the door after school and see my mother waving the tennis yearbook shouting, "You finished number thirty-five in the South!"

"Unbelievable," I shout in return. "I have never been ranked that high!"

The next day my mother calls me to the telephone. She holds it against her chest and whispers, "It's the Citadel tennis coach, Coach Boykin."

My hands shake as I pick up the phone. I clear my voice, but still, it cracks when I say hello.

"John, just calling because I got the rankings yesterday. Thirty-five in the South. That's pretty darn good."

"Thank you, I appreciate it."

This call, there is no chitchat. Instead, Coach Boykin cuts to the chase and says, "John, I'm going to be up in Greenville, South Carolina, next month. That's close to your home, right?"

"Yes, sir."

"Good, then how about I come over to your house. I got a scholarship offer I'd like you to sign."

Elated, I say, "Sure, that will be great."

When Coach Boykin arrives at our house, friends from high school fill my mother's living room. I cannot remember the last time a group of guests were invited to the house. Even more, I am stunned when my mother invites my friends into the living room.

My mother never allows anyone in the room, especially after she covered the floor in an Italian needlepoint rug. This day is special, so she's made an exception—or she's forgotten the last time I invited friends over to the house, when I was in ninth grade.

Although it was the ninth grade, it was the first time my parents allowed me to invite a group of friends to watch a movie on the television at our house. A few weeks earlier my mother had purchased a rug. When she brought it home, she continually commented that it was a Qaleen rug. She cherished this itchy wool rug with its patterns that looked more Native American than Middle Eastern. The night was perfect. My friends were having a great time. I sat on the sofa beside a girl I had a crush on. Then the evening came to an immediate stop. One of my friends was walking into the den when he tripped, sending sixteen ounces of Coca-Cola into the air and onto the rug. Once I heard the muted splat, I knew the party was over. I began cleaning the rug with a towel as fast as possible, but it was too late. My mother was in the den.

"What's going on here?"

My friends scattered into the kitchen. I sat on the floor, wanting to hide from the world. "We just spilled a little."

"Spilled what?" my mother replied with fury in her voice. "Let me see."

I removed the towel, and my mother saw the large brown cola stain.

"Oh, my goodness. What have you done to my Qaleen rug? It's ruined."

My cheeks burned with embarrassment. I wanted to run, but there was nowhere to hide. "Mom, it was just an accident." I thought to myself, *Why did I ever think this was a good idea? No one will ever want to come over again.*

She continued her rant, "Just look at this. Hand me a towel."

Like a surgical assistant in the operating room for a life-saving procedure, I handed her a towel with speed and accuracy. Before she'd finished applying cleaners and more towels, my friends had left. Alone with my mother, I watched her finish her best efforts to prevent the rug from staining.

I realized the futility of her work when she began to cry. She looked at me, curled her lips, and said, "We can never have any nice things."

All I could say was, "I am sorry, Mom. It was an accident."

The next day, a slight tan stain reminded me of the evening and before lunchtime my mother replaced the rug, keeping the stained rug rolled-up on a shelf in the garage with an assortment of other household items.

In the living room, I stand at the secretary desk, atop my mother's new Italian needlepoint rug, and introduce Coach Boykin to my friends. Next, I sit and sign the NCAA letter of intent. When I finish, I stand again and say, "Thanks to everyone for coming over today. I am excited about entering the Citadel and playing on the tennis team."

When I finish, I slowly scan the room and with a growing awareness study each face. Only two or three of my friends have seen me play tennis. My friends, many who I have known since before grammar school, remain unaware about my life as a tennis player. I have never shared with them the struggles, the grueling rides home filled with apologies and guilt, or how tennis and my need to be a compliant son consumed my existence. My life is a secret tapestry, woven with scars hidden from my friends.

They all live in the real world. I do not.

All I know is that much of my tennis life has been hearing how bad my mother's childhood had been. The world dealt her cruel blows, but she never tells me how or shares specifics. Instead, she is too busy putting her displaced passion on my shoulders and making me carry her burden.

As I realize the loss of my innocence and how I am a wandering soul looking for my own light to follow, I think to myself, *I will create a new life once I enter the Citadel.* However, I do not recognize how my voice is not in the present. Still, I am thinking of my mother, and not myself.

At the Citadel, I lose more matches during the tennis season than I win. Each match, my mother's stare through the fence pierces my spirit and weakens my inner strength. The only thing sharper than her glare are her condescending words intentionally aimed to arouse anger: "You have never played up to your talent," "Get off your ass and do something," or simply, "You are just pathetic." Once, like my brother, she even yelled out, "Stop hitting the ball like a pussy."

Each comment festers and shows me the disfigurements of my childhood. Eventually, a powder keg of emotion, I self-destruct, shouting anything in hopes of piercing my mother's armor and giving me a satisfying victory. However, nothing works. Her armor is too thick.

My mother's tactics of inflicting guilt continue, too. She knows my constant desire to be a good son has always been my greatest weakness. "Do you know how much I have sacrificed for you?" "You will never know what it is like to grow up on the mill hill with an alcoholic father," and "I am disappointed in you. All I tried to do is love you."

My teammates laugh at me, a cruel reminder of my own worthlessness and helplessness. I have nowhere to hide my shame. I have no refuge, no sanctuary other than Daniel Library, where I feed my hunger for knowledge. I cover my face with my hands and retreat inward. Once I am alone, I feel safe and cry.

I eventually quit the team in hopes of burying tennis forever. The next week, I sit in Capers Hall waiting for class to begin. My professor arrives and approaches my desk. "There is someone outside who would like to see you."

I walk out of the class and gasp. My mother stands beside the athletic director. We exchange an awkward greeting, and my mother says, "I came down here because I think you should apologize to the coach, and you ought to ask if you can come back onto the team."

I look at my mom and lower my head. Embarrassment fills my mind and body. I shrink until I feel like a tiny speck on the wall.

I give the only reply I know, "No, Mom, I don't want to quit the team." Guilt seeps from every pore.

We talk for a few minutes so she could explain how difficult it was for her to come to see me. I reply, "Thanks, Mom. I appreciate it."

"Good. Now that we have all of this settled, I am going home, and you need to be at practice today."

"Yes, ma'am."

My mother's "shoulds" and "oughts" confine me while at the same time rousing guilt.

At the end of my sophomore year, my advisor invites me to consider spending the fall semester of my junior year abroad. London, England. I dream of visiting cathedrals and experiencing museums, art galleries, and ancient libraries. My intellectual curiosity peaks. My true self breathes life.

Before I leave school for the summer, my dream is killed. Just like the false hopes of Shoals Mill, after twenty years of dedicating his life to his job at a tire manufacturing plant, my father is laid off along with 2,500 others. This includes 275 managers who are over sixty-five years old. The tire manufacturer calls it voluntary separation. The year before, it spent $1.5 billion to purchase a competitor.

Economists later claim that the 1990 recession lasted only eight months. For my family, it never ends. Layoffs are measured in dollars and cents, never pain and stress. Once upon a time, layoffs signaled leadership woes. Now, they signal strategic management, a higher stock price, and forgotten people. For me, it means two more years of playing tennis for the Citadel and ending any aspirations of studying abroad.

A week before graduating from the Citadel my mother demands I come home and study more for the LSATs. "I know what's best for you and I want you to stay close to me."

During the same week, one of my professors, Colonel Mathis, passes me in the hall. He is a Citadel alumnus from Edgefield, South Carolina. His accent is classically Southern, no twang, just the rise and fall of elongated vowels coming from the bottom of the mouth, the jaw slightly jutted, and lips pursed. He is a professor of Milton, and years later I cannot read *Paradise Lost* without hearing his voice.

He stops me in the hallway and asks, "Mr. Greenburn, you have performed exceptionally well as an English major at the Citadel, and you have expressed to me many times how you would like to become a write or continue you studies of literature. Have you given some thought to your plans for after graduating this fine institution?"

"No, sir," I reply. "Well, not exactly, sir. I am still figuring out a few things."

He nods his head and replies, "Mr. Greenburn, do not allow your modesty to hold you back."

Later that day, I visit my academic advisor. "Mr. Greenburn, have you considered applying to Harvard and continuing your literary studies?"

I respond with a blank stare and a simple, "No, sir." I say nothing more. I already know what my mother would say: "Is this your way of going off and finding yourself?"

"Mr. Greenburn, you are too modest. Your career in the department as an English major has beautifully blossomed. Your papers on melancholic figures of sixteenth-century drama are at a master's level. You should seek greater opportunities."

These last two conversations stay with me. Neither Colonel Mathis nor my advisor understands how the past has eroded my self-confidence. Like my mother, I hide it well and reluctantly trudge onward and graduate.

I share my senior thesis on Christian mysticism and T.S. Eliot's *Four Quartets* with my mother. I remind her, "The department gave me an award for my efforts." My mother reads the first page. She replies, "I do not understand it," and hands it back to me. My brother looks at me and laughs. He tells me, "Men who play the piano and study English are gay."

Inside my class ring I have inscribed a reminder: *Promises to Keep and Miles to Go Before I Sleep*. It does not matter. I am incapable of sharing my desires to write.

A month after moving back home, I arrive at the house from jogging. My mom runs and hugs me. She holds an envelope addressed to me in one hand and its contents in the other.

"You were accepted to law school," exclaims my mom. "We are so proud of you!"

I do not look at the letter or my mom. "I'm not going."

"What do you mean? Why would you not want to go? I'm planning on finding you an apartment in Columbia this weekend."

"That's why, Mom! Can't you see it? Me going to law school is what you want me to do. It's not what I want to do. I only applied to get you off my back."

A battle of emotions ensues.

I begin with the intent of remaining levelheaded and concise: "I don't see myself being happy. The graduates I know say they have crappy jobs and are unhappy. It doesn't seem like a good investment, especially if recent graduates are unhappy and wish they had chosen a different career."

She reinforces her arsenal of guilt with accusations of rebellion. This attack tries to overwhelm me with a saturation of emotions.

"You are my serendipity! Why are you rebelling like this?" She begins hyperventilating, but continues, "My heart hurts! Someone may need to take me to the hospital."

She reels about, clutching her hair, and breathing with long intentional huffs and puffs.

Her dramatic act infuriates me. I lose my patience and with heavy artillery, I yell at her, "Why don't you let me make my own choices? After all, it's my goddamn life! Jesus Christ!"

No reply. The battle, over. Her symptoms disappear. She glares and, like a dull knife says, "You no longer love me."

She turns and goes upstairs. The bedroom door slams. My father, the peacekeeper, sits in the next room. He does not follow her upstairs. He stays quiet. He knows the shame of the past is too deep to soothe.

The next day, "weary-hearted as that hollow moon," I pack my car. My dad watches. I do not look up and say, "I'll call you when I decide where I'm going."

For the first time in my life, my mother will not be there to tell me what to do.

I find a paying internship at a hospital in Spartanburg, South Carolina. The hospital allows me to live in the medical student dorms. I enjoy the companionship of the students and residents.

Later, I find my first apartment. I pay the first two months rent and the deposit. However, I do not have credit, and the lease requires the signature of a guarantor. I ask my mother. She signs it, but only after she arrives to inspect the apartment. "See, I told you that you need me. Why do you not feel the same way? Why are you running away? What have I done to you?"

The next weekend I go home to collect a few items of furniture from my room. My mom watches everything I touch. I pick up a small soapstone statue of an Asian man. She looks at me and says, "Don't take that until I see if I can use it somewhere in the house."

"But, Mom," I reply, "this has been sitting in the closet for at least two years."

"So?" she replies. "I just have not decided where to place it. Now put it back in the closet."

The next week she arrives, unannounced, at my apartment with a wooden garden bench. "Here, I thought you could use this as a couch. Enjoy it. It was expensive." Next, she brings in the Qaleen rug and says, "You need a rug, since your apartment has wood floors."

My shoulders shake with laughter when I say, "I thought this was stained. Ruined."

"Shut up," replies my mother. "No one can see it."

Two months later I sit on the bench. Below me the rug itches my bare feet. The only other furniture I own is a bed and a small table with two chairs. I look around at the empty walls. I listen to the hum of the air-conditioning unit in the window in front of me.

I answer the ringing phone.

"Mr. Greenburn, this is the University of South Carolina Law School admissions office. The semester begins in three weeks, and we have not received your information. Will you be attending?"

I read the inscription in my class ring: *Promises to Keep and Miles to Go Before I Sleep*. I hear my mother's voice.

I swallow the knot in my throat and say, "Yes, I will be there."

My father leaves the hospital room for home, hoping to find rest. I stay with my mother, studying the contours of her blank face. I gently brush her brittle gray hair, the act a tentative solace. With newfound courage, I take her hand, allowing my touch to linger, offering what small comfort I can.

She opens her eyes and looks at me with an expressionless stare. Raising my voice, I try to reach beyond her cognitive impairment. "Mom! It's me! John! I now know your past. I understand your strength. It teaches me. It shapes me. It makes me. Without it, I am incomplete. Without it, I would never be authentic."

My mother closes her eyes, and I feel her sorrow. Her history, full of pain and anguish from the mill, wraps itself around my body. Since hearing my father explain her past, I no longer feel it choking her and see the divine truth within her. I understand how her suffering had a purpose, and that purpose was to make me a better person than the corporate villains who ruined her life.

I look into the gloom, deep within myself, searching for some means by which I can make life tolerable. There, in front of me, I see how my mother's suffering has laid a path of purification, strengthening my soul.

My mother stretched me to live my best. Now, she shakes me out of my static life and into participation with the timeless. I see the true and authentic self. I hear the voice of the past calling me.

Around me, language begins to crumble, leaving only silence. The boundaries of reality vanish. Briefly, my soul is released from my body, and I see above my mother an image of our family. Each person, past, present, and future is connected to the center, like the hypnotizing silhouette of a floating snowflake.

This mystical moment is prophetic and I decide to I follow it and learn more about the past.

The following morning, I inhale the bitter antiseptic aroma of the disinfectant cleaners. They sterilize everything in the hospital room. Sometimes, we use the vastness of our imagination like a cleaning solution to sterilize our past. We want our history to be clean, like the hospital sheets that cover my mother.

I look underneath the sheets. All that remains is my mother's stained and broken body. I listen to her short, staccato breaths get shorter and faster, like a train heading down the tracks. She no longer opens her eyes. They are permanently closed and prepared for the inevitable. I look at my father holding her hand and, as if reciting a prayer, say, "Dad, it's time to call hospice. It will not be long."

He stays silent. He knows. Memories are all that remain.

My father holds my mother, lying in bed. He will hold her until her last breath.

CHAPTER TWENTY

My mother's final act is a sacred dance of departure. She arrives at the beginning in silent stillness. She awakens my consciousness. I sense my spirit is no longer hollow. I look out the window and see the hills are no longer naked and barren. Like my mended spirit they are transformed and awakened with the pulse of life.

The funeral is simple, like the pall covering the casket. Our family huddles under the Committal Shelter at the M.J. "Dolly" Cooper Veterans Cemetery. My father is proud to be a veteran, but prouder I am there with my brother and his seven grandchildren, my four, my brother's beautiful daughters who are older, the oldest with her husband.

A mockingbird sings at the top of a nearby tree. Its melody strengthens me. Each grandchild speaks about my mother. My father plays her favorite gospel songs over a portable stereo. We say the final prayer. When the service concludes, my father walks to the casket. He places his hand on the head of the casket. He whispers something to my mother he will never share.

I turn around to leave and I see a man standing in the back of the shelter. He wears a simple rumpled coat fraying on the edges. His crooked tie shows coffee and gravy stains. His shoes, worn at the heels, are torn. The man shows a familiar smile and wears his thick dark hair slicked back, like in pictures I have seen in Hazel's house.

I cautiously approach the man and say, "Good morning. Do I know you?"

The man tilts his head. One hand holds a tattered Bible. He awkwardly extends his other hand. With a definite lisp he replies, "Hi, I am Walter Craft. People call me Walt."

I shake his hand and stare into face. He wears the same blank look I have seen in the many old photographs from Shoals Mill. We share an inquisitive gaze at each other. My mouth opens, but no words come out, when suddenly Walt runs out of the shelter toward the green hillside. As he runs, he yells, "There goes Ms. Francis. Look! She is going to heaven." He points to a large tiger swallow gliding in the air, the ineffable soul of my mother floating to heaven.

After we all turn to look, Walt returns to me and smiles. "See, I finally understand Jesus."

After the funeral, we return to the house. My father guides me into the living room and opens the bottom desk drawer. I have never opened it.

"John," he says, "you need to look through this."

News clippings, pictures, and an assortment of other papers fill the drawer. There is a picture of me fishing at the pond when we first moved to the neighborhood. Another photo from the local newspaper is of me playing the piano at my ninth-grade recital; many are photos of tennis matches.

I find the Furman Music Camp concert program and a letter from Dan McGill congratulating me on my win at the Crackerland Championships held at Henry Field Stadium at the University of Georgia. There are piles of unused high school, college, graduate school, and law graduation announcements. I find a fourth-grade citizenship award and my driver's education certificate. I laugh, "Look, I think Mom saved every report card since the first grade."

For my mother everything was important, the simple and the grand. I cry. *She is gone forever.*

I continue searching through the drawer and find a yellowed stock certificate, Shoals Mill. I examine it and call my dad. "This is a stock certificate from Shoals Mill. Did you ever take this to the bank? It may have some value."

My father replies, "That abstract piece of corporate finance ain't worth a damn thing. Only real property makes a place worth living for."

I laugh and continue looking. At the bottom of the drawer, I find a ragged newspaper article. I read the headline: *Robert Henry Keyt's Remains Found on Island in Lake.*

1960: A group of high school kids exploring an island on Lake Hartwell have found the remains of Robert Henry Keyt. His remains lay beside the marked graves of his father, John Williams, his mother, Ella, and his brother, James. Bedside the body lay a rusted pistol.

After a brief investigation, the coroner ruled the cause of death suicide.

Many of South Carolina's man-made lakes, formed by damming rivers, caused the relocation of several towns and homes. The remnants are still below the water, visible only to divers. A few places remain above water. One such place, the former Keyt family farm, was repossessed and sold to the state to make way for the lake.

During the construction of the lake no one moved the Keyt family graves. The government washed its hands stating, "The graves are set on the highest point of the old farm and remain above the waterline. As a result, there was no need to move them."

The county coroner office assisted with the burial of Robert Henry's remains in a marked grave beside the family.

I take the stock certificate and the news article and walk into the kitchen. My dad is sitting at the table, sipping a cup of coffee. I show him both and ask, "Dad, why did Mom keep these in the same drawer as my stuff?"

My father's eyes gleam as he replies, "She knew you would want to know."

CHAPTER TWENTY-ONE

It is hard to think about going back to my house in Florida. Although I have lived in three different states in the past twenty years, upstate South Carolina has always been home. I love the scenery, the history, the people, and most of all, the memories. Here, people have celebrated special times with me, and most importantly, they have always loved and supported me. This will always be my home.

Regardless, I must return to Florida, where my life sits, waiting in the shadows. I wrestle with my own transformation. *Why must I go back? No one will understand this transcendental experience I have achieved. This is what truly defines me.* As my mind fills with reluctance, I think back to my dream of the river.

I close my eyes and feel the pulse of the water against my body. I begin to understand why the past does not die. It is forever a part of our experience, and we cannot disown it. It lives within us, and we must embrace it if we are to understand. With this gift of clarity, I hear the voice of my calling and know I must return to Cogniv-Pharma and face the ending.

Before we leave town there is one more piece of my past I must show my family. We drive over to Shoals Mill. As we cross over the railroad tracks, Mary says, "Dad, what happened to your grandparents' house?"

The children look down Park Avenue and see only a grassy knoll. I reply, "I do not know. Obviously, someone felt it was time to tear it down."

I drive until I find the ball field. From the back seat I hear, "Dad, why are we stopping here?"

"Let's get out and I'll show you." We all walk over to the ball field, where the fence leans to the ground. Although the field's lights still stand tall, the light bulbs are all shattered. We walk through the tall weeds covering what was once the outfield.

I see a tick on my leg. I flick it off. Past the outfield fence, I see a granite marker resting in a clear spot. Still standing. *Fireball still refuses to forget, too.*

Only Henry has seen the marker. He leans over and reads aloud the marker's inscription: *To Henry, for his dedication and unselfish effort in helping… He instilled in all who ever played for him the will to win. His greatest victory was the victory over sin through Jesus Christ.*

Henry looks at me with a wide grin and says, "Dad, take a picture of me with the marker."

Henry will never forget, and neither will my family.

I return to the dark domain of the corporate boardroom. Greedy men of power, whose cold determinism forbids free will, surround the polished mahogany table. The even darker stained walls hide decisions of corruption.

Mr. Arden walks in with a ranging stride. He sits and fixes his tie to show off his diamond cuff links. He clears his throat, adjusts his tailored suit jacket, and pounds the gavel. All of this act is an effort to display his power and wealth.

As he calls the meeting to order someone interrupts, "Where is Mrs. Verity?"

Mr. Arden scowls and cracks his knuckles. In a voice filled with hubris he says, "She is no longer on the board."

He casts a slow, powerful gaze over the room, reminding everyone present of his control.

I look around the cold, monotone boardroom. Each director sits in a black leather chair, wearing a dark suit, white starched shirt, and shiny red silk necktie. Their appearance confirms allegiance to Mr. Graves.

During the meeting men talk about profits and market share as they listen to reports offered by the chief financial officer and chief strategy officer. I do not listen. Instead, my mind wanders. I think about how I missed the warning signs, or at least did not take them seriously, when I began working at Cogniv-Pharma, comments about how federal regulations require a compliance officer and how it is a "necessary evil." Other comments labeled my position in the company as "a symbolic position made to appease the government." Worse, a few said, "It's not something we want. It's a mandated requirement from government."

I sit, almost stunned, looking at my report about the subpoena. I now understand how my role was never intended to be an executive position with more responsibility and autonomy. Instead, my seat at the table is a charade, a simple prison devoid of freedom and liberty for me.

During the meeting I do not act. I only observe. I listen to the conversations and appreciate how each man around the boardroom table is full conceit. Their lives are nothing more than callous machinations inspired by greed for money and fame.

My intellect, desperate for deeper knowledge, seeks new directions to spark my curiosity. However, curiosity, the engine of intellectual achievement, no longer exists for me. These men of action, who now surround me, attempt to erode the truth my mother has shown me.

At the close of the board meeting, but prior to asking for a motion to adjourn, Mr. Arden announces, "Ladies and gentlemen! May I have your attention? We need to enter into an executive session with the chief ethics officer. No others may be present so that we may have a candid conversation with Mr. Greenburn, about his report and recommendations regarding a recent subpoena.

Mr. Arden convenes the executive session. I know he does not respect me. He uses his primal instincts to isolate me like a lion stalking the weakest member of the herd. He stands over the table. "Now, everyone has read the report from the chief ethics officer found in the board agenda." He deliberately stares at me, his voice now sardonic. "Would anyone like to speak about it?"

A rhetorical question.

Yet, he underestimates my quiet strength. I still have one last maneuver he does not anticipate.

The chairman turns the page of the board agenda. "Since there are no questions, I will read the recommended action item from the compliance officer for us to consider."

Action Item
The board of directors should direct management to fully cooperate with the Department of Justice by expeditiously collecting and providing all information requested in the subpoena.

Mr. Arden's fortune and fame have been built on the profits of the company he chairs. He knows prison hangs in the balance but has escaped the labyrinth of the judicial system many times. As a major player in politics, he lives in a tangled web of compromised moral principles centered on personal entitlement.

Mr. Arden's power has been amassed by leaving no survivors. His sole motivation is always protecting only himself. An undercurrent of perverse rumors surrounds his past.

"Gentlemen," commands Mr. Arden, "let me begin." The directors acknowledge him with a simple nod.

Still standing, Mr. Arden commences: "I have talked to our attorney. He agrees with me that we are doing the same thing that every other pharmaceutical manufacturer is doing, has always done, and always will. As a result, he recommends the company fight this subpoena with an arsenal of motions aimed at squashing this ridiculous intervening by government."

I feel the tension in the room. Directors shift in their chairs. A few clear their throats. They know the right thing to do. Regardless, I know they will not cross Mr. Arden.

Mr. Arden continues, "Now, why in hell should we approve this recommended action by the chief ethics officer?"

A director, a friend and neighbor of Mr. Arden, speaks up, "But I thought we established the role of chief ethics officer to be independent and not subordinate to legal counsel?"

Mr. Arden looks across the table. His voice snarls, "Like me, don't you own your own business?"

"I do."

"And who do you call when you have legal trouble?"

"I call my attorney."

"Exactly!" roars Mr. Arden. "You call your attorney, not some damn chief ethics officer who is going to recommend something to just make you feel good about yourself."

I think, *Intimidation and corruption are the deepest realms of noir.*

Mr. Arden's ruddy cheeks darken. His predatory instincts on the attack. He explains how chief ethics officers, like me, graduate from third-tier law schools. "I don't even believe it is an accredited school." He shows my bar examination results—two tries before passing. "Gentlemen, lawyers who struggle to pass the bar become ethics officers, not attorneys."

The directors nod in agreement. I remain stoic, a coping mechanism I learned at an early age. I think of my mother, and, in a strange way, this helps me remain composed. She gives me peace.

Mr. Arden, sensing victory, finishes: "Now, who would you trust? Our esteemed attorney, who has always been by our side, or a chief ethics officer who has never practiced law?"

Their minds are too Machiavellian. Internally, they acquit themselves. Management will suffer the burden of these actions, not the board.

Greed, a deformation of the soul, is a human disease blurring life's purpose into an insatiable pursuit of wealth and power. It destroyed the mill and its way of life. In many ways, it destroyed my mother, too. As the board of directors vote against my recommendation, noting their strong desire to fight the subpoena, I realize they are following the same path. *It will also destroy Cogniv-Pharma.*

After the board meeting, I sit still. My current adult life, overtaken by a cold corporate existence, has existed as a shadow in the shade. It has been a life filled with workaholism, perfectionism, and chameleon-type behavior, which sadly leads me back to the pain of my past.

Next, I think of my mother, our time at the hospital, and her funeral.

I will no longer be embarrassed to submit to the genius of my heart. I will no longer cower when the specters of the past call to me in the still darkness of morning, hushing the hooting owl into slumber. Instead, I will embrace the past with open arms and fully learn what it is built upon.

Near the end of my twelve-month respite from corporate America, I have no desire to return. During this time, my family celebrated my mother's life by spending several weeks in Europe, including a riverboat cruise down the Danube on which we are joined by my father.

Now, back from our European trip, I sit in my office at home contemplating how to begin finding out more about my mother's past, when Clare calls me to the den. "John, come quick and see what's on the news." I hold little interest in what is happening in today's world, but still mosey into the den.

I look at the television and a bolt of shock opens my eyes wide. Susie from the Pinnacle Club is on the television. She holds a crying baby and says to the news reporter, "I didn't know what else to do when Mr. Arden refused to acknowledge our baby."

Just like Marlowe Rex.

I at once recall the party when Susie slipped in the back door of Mr. Graves's office. *So, that was why she was there.*

The news story comes back from a commercial break and begins again, "Mistress Aids Department of Justice Investigation into the Actions of Cogniv-Pharma and Receives a $10 Million Award."

I look at Clare in disbelief as the news story continues, "Both the CEO, Mr. Graves, and the Chairman, Mr. Arden, used payments from their respective family foundations and illegally influenced physicians to hide documentation of postsurgical complications associated with Cogniv-Pharma's most popular drug, RemMem."

After I left Mr. Graves's office during the party Susie must have taken the documents I had found and left on the desk. I still have never told Clare and never will. Maybe it's better to leave some things where they lie, in the past.

After hearing the story, I go outside to my backyard. The hairy stems of the butterfly weed are bare. Caterpillars have eaten the leaves. The chrysalises underneath the garden are transparent and empty. Transformation has occurred, but farther underneath the shed hangs a new row of sea-foam green chrysalises. More transformation awaits.

For now, each day, I enjoy looking at the horizon and watching a child and his mother walk hand in hand past the Cardinal Racquet Club, past the tennis courts at the Citadel, and over the hill into the sunset.

ABOUT THE AUTHOR

MICHAEL SPAKE was born and raised in Anderson, South Carolina, a town deeply rooted in the textile industry. Two generations of his father's family were employed at Brogan Mill, also known as Appleton Mill. They were characterized by their dedication and resilience, embracing life's challenges on the mill with steadfast resolve. Michael's paternal grandfather, Henry "Grinny" Spake, became a beloved figure in the community, positively impacting many lives through his involvement as a youth sports coach.

Michael's passion for tennis began at age five, learning by hitting a ball against the side of his family's home and later at the Cardinal Racquet Club. He received formal coaching from Jim Boykin, a renowned coach at Anderson College and later the University of North Carolina at Charlotte. A standout athlete, Michael was a six-year letterman at T.L. Hanna High School, where his team claimed the AAA State Championship in 1986, 1987, and 1988. He continued his athletic journey and became a four-year letterman at The Citadel, earning the prestigious Marion S. Lewis Tennis Award twice. This annual honor is bestowed upon the player deemed to have made the greatest contribution to The Citadel's tennis program, as determined by the team and coaches.

Currently residing in Lakeland, Florida, Michael serves as the Chief Compliance and Integrity Officer and Senior Vice President of External Affairs for a prominent health system in Central Florida. A respected thought leader in healthcare management and compliance, Michael is a published author on these subjects and has also held adjunct faculty positions at several universities and colleges.

In addition to his professional accomplishments, Michael is a writer of Southern fiction. His recently published short stories delve into the distinctive characters and landscapes of his native South Carolina. His debut novel, Life Close to the Bone, explores the intricate interplay between the past and the present, delving into themes of understanding and connection.

Michael has been married to Mary Lucia Spake for 28 years, and together, they have four children: Henry, Mary Clare, Kathryn, and Vivian. In his leisure time, he enjoys nurturing his backyard butterfly garden, caring for his hens, and embracing the simple joys of life with his family and their two dogs, Hazel and Harley.